# Die For Me

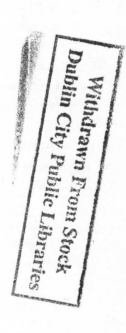

# Die For Me

*Luke Jennings*

JOHN MURRAY

First published in Great Britain in 2020 by John Murray (Publishers)
An Hachette UK company

1

Copyright © Luke Jennings 2020

A CIP catalogue record for this title is available from the British Library

Hardback ISBN 9781529351514
Trade Paperback ISBN 9781529351521
eBook ISBN 9781529351545

Typeset in Sabon MT by Hewer Text UK Ltd, Edinburgh
Printed and bound in Great Britain by Clays Ltd, Elcograf S.p.A.

John Murray policy is to use papers that are natural, renewable
and recyclable products and made from wood grown in sustainable
forests. The logging and manufacturing processes are expected to
conform to the environmental regulations of the country of origin.

John Murray (Publishers)
Carmelite House
50 Victoria Embankment
London EC4Y 0DZ

www.johnmurraypress.co.uk

for the clowns

I

As the light fades, an icy wind rises. A south-easterly, racing out of the Gulf of Riga across the Baltic Sea and meeting the ship broadside, so that the containers groan and strain against their lashing rods. Every day, as we voyage eastward towards Russia, the temperature falls.

The container that Villanelle and I have shared for the last five days is a corrugated steel box the size of a prison cell. It's a little over two and a half metres tall, contains a part-load of clothing bales, and sits atop a five-container stack on the starboard side of the ship. Inside, it's as cold as death. The two of us live like rats, huddling together for warmth, nibbling at our diminishing stock of stale bread, cheese and chocolate, sipping our rationed water, and urinating into a plastic bucket. I've been constipated since the ship left port on the north-east coast of England, and Villanelle shits into a series of plastic bags bought from a pet shop, which she then neatly knots and stores.

At the forward end of the container there's an emergency hatch, perhaps thirty centimetres by thirty, which can be unbolted from the inside. This admits a thin shaft of light and a freezing blast of salt air. Standing on the clothing bales, my eyes streaming, I watch the steady rise and fall of

1

the horizon and the slow-motion leap of the bow wave, white against grey, until my face loses all feeling. When the wind drops, I'll pour the piss-bucket out of the hatch. It'll freeze as it runs down the container. I've asked Villanelle to throw her shit bags out too, but she's worried that one might land on deck.

She's thought of everything. Thermal vests and leggings, underwear, toilet paper, washing stuff, tampons, neoprene gloves, red-light torches, a commando knife, plasticuffs, 9mm ammunition for her Sig Sauer and my Glock, and a hefty roll of used US dollars. We have no phones, laptops or credit cards. No identifying documents. Nothing to leave a trail. No one except Villanelle knows for certain that I'm alive, and Villanelle is officially dead herself. Her grave, marked with a small metal plaque provided by the Russian state and inscribed Оксана Воронцова, is in the Industrialny cemetery in Perm.

Two years ago I didn't know that Villanelle, or Oxana Vorontsova, existed.

I was in charge of a small inter-Service liaison depart-ment at Thames House, MI5's London headquarters, and life was, on balance, fine. Work was on the dull side: I had an MA in criminology and forensic psychology, and had hoped for a more challenging deployment with the Security Service. On the positive side I had a steady if unspectacular income, and my husband Niko was a kind and decent man whom I loved, and with whom I was hoping to start a family. There were worse things, I told myself, than routine, and if I spent every spare moment at the office building up a file of unattributed political assassinations, it was just a private thing. Just me keeping my hand in. A hobby, really.

In the course of this unofficial research I became convinced that several of these killings had been carried out by a woman, and almost certainly by the same woman. Normally, I would have kept this theory to myself. My role at MI5 was administrative, not investigative, and there would have been raised eyebrows and condescending smiles if I'd brought the subject up with my superiors. I'd have been regarded as a slow-lane liaison officer getting above herself. Then a Russian far-right political activist named Viktor Kedrin was shot dead at a London hotel, along with his three bodyguards. I was accused of failing to organise adequate protection for Kedrin, and fired.

This was bitterly unjust and everyone involved knew it. But we also knew that when the department fouled up as royally as this, and it didn't get much worse than the assassination of a high-profile principal like Kedrin, someone had to take the fall. Ideally, someone senior enough to count, but not so senior that they couldn't easily be replaced. Someone expendable. Someone like me.

Shortly after I'd cleared my desk and handed in my pass at Thames House, I was discreetly contacted by a long-serving MI6 officer named Richard Edwards who, unlike his counterparts north of the river, was prepared to listen to my ideas. Seconded to his off-the-books team, and tasked with finding Kedrin's killer, I pursued Villanelle around the world. She proved a spectral and elusive quarry, always one flawless step ahead. All I could do was follow the blood trail. And, unwillingly, admire her grim artistry. She was bold, free from guilt or fear, and probably a little bored by the ease with which she evaded detection. Flattered to discover that I was pursuing her, Villanelle began to do the same to me. One night in Shanghai, she climbed up the outside of my hotel into my room and stole my bracelet as a trophy. To make amends, and for the sheer effrontery of it, she broke into my house in London in broad daylight, to leave me a different (and much more expensive) bracelet that she'd bought for me in Venice. These intrusions were as flirtatious as they were terrifying. Whispered reminders that she liked me, but could kill me at any time she chose.

Although I refused to admit it at the time, even to myself, this twisted courtship had its effect. Obsession is not immediate. It stalks you. It creeps up on you until it's too late to escape it. When I first saw Villanelle in person it was by chance, and again it was in Shanghai. I was on a scooter, caught in traffic, and she was walking down the pavement towards me, dressed entirely in black, with her blonde hair slicked back from her face. Our eyes met, and I knew it was her. Villanelle can be sweetness itself when she chooses, but that evening her gaze was as flat as a snake's. She claims that she recognised me on that occasion, just as I recognised her, but I don't believe her. She lies. She lies compulsively, all the time. Later that night she lured my colleague Simon Mortimer into an alleyway and hacked him to death with a meat-cleaver. The savagery of the attack shocked seasoned investigators of the Shanghai homicide squad, who had seen their share of Triad killings and other horrors.

Our second meeting, on the hard shoulder of a motorway in England, was orchestrated with chilling brilliance. I was driving back to London from a Security Services interrogation centre in Hampshire. My passenger was Dennis Cradle, a senior MI5 officer who, earlier that morning, had admitted to me that he was in the pay of the Twelve, the organisation that employed Villanelle to do their killing. I'd tried to turn Cradle, to get him to inform on the Twelve in return for immunity, and he'd responded by trying to recruit me, which was pretty fucking cheeky, all things considered.

Twenty minutes into the journey, we were flagged down by a female police officer on a motorcycle. It was Villanelle, of course, but by the time I'd figured that out, it was too late. Villanelle told me that she'd missed me. Touched my hair, and talked about my 'pretty eyes'. It was all rather romantic, in its way. Then she disabled my car and abducted Cradle, leaving me stranded beside the motorway. Cradle probably thought he was being rescued. In fact, Villanelle drove him to a secluded spot outside Weybridge, smashed the back of his skull with a blunt instrument – I'm guessing a police-issue baton – and dumped him in the River Wey.

Villanelle wasn't ideal girlfriend material, but then I wasn't looking for a girlfriend. I was married, for heaven's sake. Happily married, to a man. And if sex with Niko had never been transcendent – no flaring comet-trails or exploding supernovae, no werewolf howls – I had no complaints. He was that rarest of beings, a genuinely good guy. He loved me when no one else gave me a second glance. He praised my hopeless cooking, was enchanted by my fashion-blindness, and regularly assured me, in the teeth of evidence to the contrary, that I was beautiful. In return, I treated him appallingly. I knew exactly how much I was going to hurt him, and I did it anyway.

It was the way Villanelle made me feel. For all my frozen horror at what she had done, I was awestruck. Her focus, her meticulousness, her ruthless purity of purpose. I'd been sleepwalking through life and suddenly there she was, my perfect adversary.

I would learn later that Villanelle had felt the same way. That while working as the Twelve's star assassin had its professional and material rewards, she had begun to crave an excitement that routine political murders didn't deliver. She had developed an appetite for danger. She wanted to lure a pursuer onto her trail, someone worthy of her mettle. She wanted to dance on the razor's edge. She wanted me.

Niko loved me, and I'd always felt safe in his arms, but the games that Villanelle played were satanically addictive. It took Simon's murder to awaken me to the boundless range of her psychopathy. I hated her after that, which was what she intended. She wanted to show me the worst of herself, to see if I'd back off. Of course I only came after her all the harder, which delighted her, but then Villanelle never drew any distinction between hate and desire, between pursuit and courtship, and in the end, neither did I.

When did I lose perspective? Was it in Venice, when I discovered that she'd been there a month earlier with another woman, a lover, and I found myself transfixed with jealousy? Or was it earlier, by the side of the motorway, when she told me that after climbing into my hotel room on that monsoon night in Shanghai, she'd sat and gazed at me as I slept? It doesn't matter any more. What matters is that when Villanelle asked me to come with her, to walk out of my life and leave behind everything and everyone I'd ever known, I did so without hesitation.

I knew, by then, that I'd been living a lie. That from the time I'd first been approached by Richard Edwards, I'd been brilliantly, artfully deceived. When Richard asked me to investigate Villanelle and the Twelve I flattered myself that he was impressed by my intuitive and deductive skills. In fact he'd been a fully paid-up asset of the Twelve all along, and wanted to use me to test the organisation's security. It was a classic false flag operation, and by conducting it off the books, for reasons that made perfect sense to me at the time, he ensured that no one at MI6 got wind of it.

I had begun to suspect that I'd been used in this way, but it was Villanelle who finally confirmed it. She's a psychopath and a habitual liar, but she was the only one who told me the truth. She showed me, dispassionately, just how easily I'd been manipulated. Listening to her was like watching an elaborate stage set being dismantled, and suddenly seeing ropes and pulleys and raw brickwork. She told me that she'd been given her next target, and that it was me. I'd discovered more than I was meant to. I wasn't the Twelve's dupe any longer, I was a liability.

The encounter, and its aftermath, was classic Villanelle. I'd just returned from a horrendous few days in Moscow, and when I got back to my flat I found her in the bath, washing her hair. A 9mm Sig Sauer was lying between the taps, and she was wearing latex gloves. I was pretty sure she meant to shoot me. Villanelle is coy about how many people she's killed. She just says 'normal amount', but I'd guess that the figure is nineteen, maybe twenty victims.

We had to stage my death. Then we had to disappear.

So that's what we did, and soon we were racing through the night on her Ducati motorcycle, my arms wrapped tightly around her, heading north. Villanelle didn't really give me a choice, but then I didn't want her to. I was ready to cut the ground from beneath me. I was ready to fly.

I've often wondered, since that day, what would have happened if I'd stayed. If I'd begged Niko's forgiveness, and gone to the police, or perhaps even the newspapers, with my story. Would I have survived? Or would it have been the car that didn't stop, the heart-attack on the way to the supermarket, the apparent suicide? And if the Twelve had finally decided that I wasn't worth killing, and had engineered things so that I looked and sounded like a conspiracy theorist, just one more recruit to the sad, twilight army of the deluded, would Niko ever have trusted me? Or would I have forever felt his eyes on me, watching and wondering, as we made small talk over dinner, or endured endless evenings at the bridge club?

We stowed away at Immingham, a port in Lincolnshire. It cost us the motorcycle and the remains of my dignity. The guy was a deckhand, on shore with a crew visa. We hooked up with him in a pub outside the terminal, a fake Irish establishment so depressing it was almost funny. We'd been nursing a couple of beers for the best part of an hour when the guy came in. Villanelle clocked him as Russian straight away, swung over to his table, and went to work. His name was Igor and his ship, as we'd hoped, was the *Kirovo-Chepetsk*, a Panamax-class container vessel bound for St Petersburg. Villanelle didn't waste any time. Poured a treble vodka into him and made her pitch. Igor didn't look too surprised.

When we took him outside to see the bike, it had started snowing. Villanelle unzipped the waterproof cover, and Igor gave a low whistle. I don't know one end of a motorcycle from the other, but the Ducati was a thing of beauty and riding on it behind Villanelle had been a dream.

'Want to try her out?' Villanelle asked, her breath vaporous. Igor nodded, slowly running his hands over the handlebar controls and the volcano-grey tank. Then he swung a leg over the saddle, thumbed the ignition switch, and took off on a whisper-quiet circuit of the car park, snowflakes whirling in the headlight beam. When he dismounted, clearly smitten, Villanelle pressed home her advantage in fast, idiomatic Russian. He answered in a murmur, shifting his weight uneasily.

'He'll get us on board tomorrow night,' she said. 'But the bike's not going to be enough. He'll do prison time if he's caught.'

'What else does he want?'

'He wants to see your . . .' She nodded at my chest.

'My . . . *No*. No way!'

'Just one photo, for his private use. He says you remind him of his Aunty Galya.'

'Are you fucking kidding me?'

'No. She drives a tram in Smolensk. Get them out.'

I looked around the car park. There was no one, except for the three of us. Unzipping my leather bike jacket, I pulled up my sweater, thermal vest and bra. Fuck, it was cold.

Staring, Igor fumbled in his track bottoms for his phone. It took him the best part of a minute of crouching and weaving to get the shot he wanted.

'Just make sure my face isn't in the picture,' I said, shivering. Snow was blurring the lenses of my glasses.

'He's not interested in your face. He says you have nice breasts, though. And I agree.'

'Well it's nice that you're both having such a lovely time, but I'm literally freezing my tits off here. Can I please get dressed?'

'Yeah, we're good. He'll help us.'

'When do they load this container onto the ship?' I whispered, as we hollowed ourselves out a nest in the clothing bales.

'Tomorrow, the driver said. Probably around midday.'

'Do you think anyone will check inside first?'

'They might. Are you afraid?'

'Right now, I just don't want us to be caught.'

She said nothing.

'How long have you been planning this?' I said.

'I've always known that one day things might change and I might have to run. So I worked out escape routes. What I didn't plan for was you coming too.'

'Sorry about that.'

'It's OK. Your spoken Russian is shit, so when we get to St Petersburg you can be mute. Maybe weak in the head. Maybe both. Take your leathers and boots off.'

'Why?'

'So you have something to put on tomorrow when you wake up. Also we have to keep each other warm, share body heat. Do what I say.'

'Please,' I said.

'Please what?'

'Please do what I say.'

She jerked herself away from my side. 'Fuck "please", *suchka*. You want to stay alive, you obey me.'

'I see.'

'Obviously you don't see. This is my world, OK?'

'It's mine too, now. Whether I want it or not.'

'You want to leave? Fine. See how long you last, *yebanutaya*.'

I couldn't see her. But I sensed her fury, radiating through the darkness.

'Villanelle,' I began. 'Oxana—'

'Don't *ever* call me that.'

'OK, I'm sorry, but—'

'But nothing, Polastri. I hope you freeze. I mean it, I hope you fucking die.'

I undid my jacket, trousers and boots and placed them where I could find them in the dark. Beside me, I could hear Villanelle doing the same. Shivering, I settled myself into the bales, about a metre away from her. As the minutes crept by, and the cold wrapped more and more tightly around me, I listened to the calm rise and fall of her breathing. Hateful bitch.

What was I doing? Why, knowing everything that I knew, had I trusted her? I clamped my teeth together, but was unable to prevent them chattering. I pressed my hand over my mouth, blinking away tears of hopeless, abject fury, and knew that I'd destroyed everything in my life that had value. That I'd ignored the inner voice that might have saved me, and thrown in my lot with an unfeeling monster who killed people without a second thought, and who would probably, sooner or later, kill me.

I wiped my nose with my sleeve, and sniffed. A heartbeat later I felt Villanelle shift. She moulded herself against me, her knees behind mine, her breasts against my back. Nudging my hair out of the way with her nose, she pressed her face against my neck. Then she folded her arm over mine and arranged her fingers around my wrist. I was still shivering, and she moved more closely against me.

Finally, as the warmth of her body possessed me, I was still. Silence enclosed us, and I imagined the snow beating at the container's walls and roof. My arm twitched, as it sometimes does at night, and Villanelle's hand closed around mine, her thumb firm in my palm. Taking a tress of my hair between her teeth she gently tweaked it, then licked the nape of my neck as if she were a lioness. And bit me, hard.

I arched away from her, gasping, but she grabbed my shoulders, swung me onto my back, and pulled herself on top of me so that we were face to face in the darkness, her breath beer-sour, her nose cold against my cheek. Then her tongue was in my mouth, snaking and probing. I twisted my head away. 'Stop.'

'Why?'

'Just . . . talk to me.'

She rolled onto her side. 'What about?'

'Have you ever really cared, really *felt* anything, for another person?'

'You think I can't feel?'

'I don't know. Can you?'

'I feel like you feel, Eve. I'm not some freak.' She took my hand and pulled it into her pants. 'Feel my pussy. Wet.'

It was. I left my hand there for a single, dizzying heart-beat. 'That's not the same as caring about someone,' I heard myself say.

'It's a good start.'

I steadied my breath. 'So have you ever been in love?'

12

'Mmm . . . Sort of. Once.'

'And?'

'She didn't want me.'

'How did you feel?'

'I wanted to kill myself. To show her.'

'So where am I, in all of this?'

'You're here, dumbass. With me.' Her fingers found my hair. 'And if you don't kiss me right now, I really am going to kill you.' She started to pull me towards her, but I was already there, searching for her mouth with mine.

Then we were all over each other, bumping noses, smearing lips, and blindly, desperately kissing. I felt her fingers hook into the waistbands of my thermal leggings and pants and drag them over my ankles, and as she moved back up my body I tried to pull her sweater off, but the neck was so tight that she fell on top of me, laughing and whispering that I was choking her. Sitting astride me, she inched the sweater forwards over her head. It brushed my face – warm wool, stale sweat – and then it was gone, and her vest and bra after it. She pulled mine off and I shuddered as the cold seized me. 'We need to toughen you up, *pupsik*,' she whispered, wriggling out of her own leggings and pants.

All was rapt discovery. Her skin and my skin, her smell and my smell, her mouth and my mouth. Villanelle took charge, as I needed her to, and I felt her hand reach confidently between my thighs. She'd killed a man with a knife-thrust through the femoral artery. A strike so delicate, so surgically precise, that her victim was probably not immediately aware that he'd been stabbed. Could she feel the throbbing of my femoral artery? When she slid those fingers inside me, was she remembering other, bloodier penetrations? Did

13

the warm explorations of her tongue recall more lethal partings of flesh?

Afterwards we pulled our sweaters and jackets on top of us, and I folded into her back, spoonwise. For several minutes I lay there in the dark, overwhelmed, my lips touching the soft hair on her neck, which stirred as I breathed.

'It's weird,' she said. 'I can't remember what you look like.'

'Not at all?'

'No. You could be anyone.'

I raised myself on one elbow. 'Why do you like me? Truthfully?'

'Who says I like you?'

'Don't you?'

'Maybe. Maybe I just wanted to get into your pants. Which, by the way, are not pretty.'

'Ah.'

She wriggled her bottom against me. 'Truthfully, I have a thing for dorky women. Especially in glasses.'

'Thank you so much.'

'*Pozhaluysta*. I need to pee.'

She did so, noisily, into the bucket, which she'd lodged in the clothing bales in one corner. I followed her there and did the same, not easy in the dark, then we dressed ourselves – it was just too cold not to – and I curled up behind her again, with the sharp smell of her hair in my face. 'Admit it, *pupsik*,' she murmured, barely audible, 'this is a much more romantic honeymoon than your first one.'

We woke the next morning as the truck shuddered into life and began its journey to the docks. We lay motionless, the only sound the slopping of the urine in the bucket.

Twenty minutes later we came to a halt, and I felt Villanelle's body relax and her breathing become slow and calm. This was the moment of maximum danger. If there was to be an inspection of the container and its cargo, it would be now. I tried to imitate Villanelle's zen state, but started to tremble uncontrollably. My heart was pounding so wildly I thought I was going to pass out.

A dull clang reverberated throughout the container. I burrowed desperately into the bales, ignoring a brief explosion of pain as my nose struck Villanelle's forehead or shoulder. The truck began to move again, but I stayed submerged, inhaling the thick smell of unaired cotton. This time the journey was shorter, our stop–start progress indicating that we were in a line of vehicles approaching the loading bay. With the final halt, the truck's engine fell silent. There was a harsh scraping of metal on metal, a heavy thump, and we started to ascend. I'd dreaded the moment the container was hoisted from shore to ship, picturing it swinging sickeningly beneath the cranes. Nothing of the sort happened, of course. The process was smooth and deft, with only a brief kiss of steel to indicate the moment we were locked in place, and a faint knocking as our temporary home was fixed to those beneath it.

Hours passed, during which the smell of urine grew stronger, and Villanelle maintained an unapproachable, trance-like silence. Was she telling herself that she'd made a fatal miscalculation in bringing me with her? Had the previous night meant nothing to her at all? I lay there, staring into the cold darkness. Finally I slept.

I woke to the steady thrum of the *Kirovo-Chepetsk*'s engines and the faint creak of the containers around us. As

15

I regained my bearings, Villanelle's hand reached through the darkness and found mine.

'Are you OK?' she whispered.

I nodded, still not quite there.

'Hey. We're alive. We got away.'

'For now.'

'Now's all there is, *pupsik*.' She pressed my palm to her icy cheek. 'Now's all there ever is.'

# 2

I'm beginning to learn Villanelle's ways.

She withdraws. She locks herself into the secret citadel of her mind. I'm sitting there next to her, her leg warm against mine, our breath mingling, but she could be a thousand miles away, so arctic is her solitude. Sometimes it happens when we lie down to sleep and she burrows into me for warmth. Part of her is just not there. I long to tell her that she's not alone, but the truth is that she's utterly alone.

This frozen state can last for hours, and then, like dawn breaking, she'll wake to my presence. At these times I've learnt to wait and see which way the cat jumps, because she's so unpredictable. Sometimes she's pensive, just wanting to be held, sometimes she's as sullen and spiteful as a child. When she wants sex, she reaches for me. After four days and nights at sea, this has become a raw, feral business. We need the water that we have for drinking, washing is impossible, and our bodies are rank. Not that either of us cares. Villanelle knows what she wants and goes straight for it, and with the last of my inhibitions dispelled by the darkness and the desperate uncertainty of our situation, I'm soon giving as good as I get. Villanelle likes this. She's much stronger than me, and could easily throw me off when I pin her down and roll on top of her, but she lets it happen, and lies there as I stroke her breast, and my tongue and my teeth probe for the scar tissue on her lip. And then she grabs my hand and pulls it downwards, cramming my fingers inside her, and grinds against the heel of my palm until she's gasping, and sometimes laughing, and I can feel the muscles of her thighs twitching and shuddering.

'You've never been with another woman?' she says. 'I'm really your first?'

This is a conversation we've had before. 'You know I am,' I tell her.

'I don't *know*.'

'Sweetie, take my word for it. You're the first.'

'Mmm.'

'I thought about it a lot. What it would be like with you. What we might do.'

'That's what you were doing in that shitty office all day? Thinking of having sex with me?'

'I was mostly trying to catch you, if you remember. An entire MI6 team was trying to catch you.'

'You never got close, *pupsik*. What were they called, those losers you worked with?'

'Billy and Lance.'

'That's right. Billy and Lance. Did you think about having sex with them?'

'Literally never. Billy was a computer wonk who lived with his mum, and Lance was a bit like a rat. A super-cunning, well-trained rat, but still, you know . . .'

'A rat?'

'Exactly.'

She considers this for a moment. 'You know that when I was bored, in Paris, I used to hack your computer.'

'You did tell me that, yes.'

'It wasn't interesting. Ever. I hoped to find emails from a lover or whatever. But it was just orders for bin-liners and moth traps and awful, ugly clothes.'

'Sorry. That's called life.'

'Life doesn't have to be so sad. You don't have to buy acrylic sweaters, for example. Even moths think they're disgusting.'

'You kill people for a living and you're criticising my knitwear?'

'It's not the same thing, Eve. Clothes matter. And what's Rinse-Aid? Is it for your hair? Some kind of charitable organisation?'

'Sweetie, have you never used a dishwasher?'

'No. Why?'

I kiss her nose. 'It doesn't matter.'

'And now you're laughing at me. Again.'

'I'm not. Really I'm not.'

Her breathing slows. 'I could have killed you, Eve. So easily. But I didn't. I saved your life, and I risked my own, which to be very honest with you was a fucking stupid thing to do. But because I care for you, I got you away from London, and the Twelve, and that asshole husband you never loved, and I'm taking you to my country. So what do you do? You laugh at me because I don't know what fucking Rinse-Aid is.'

'Sweetie, I'm—'

'Don't call me "Sweetie". I'm not your sweetie and you're not mine. You know my girlfriend is in a Moscow prison because of you?'

'If you mean Larissa Farmanyants, she's hardly there because of me. She tried to shoot me in a crowded Metro station, missed, killed a harmless old man, and got herself arrested.'

'And now she's locked up in Butyrka. Well, you know what? I wish you were there and Lara was here. She used to lick my pussy for hours on end. She had the most powerful jaws of any woman I ever met, like a pit bull.'

'She sounds adorable.'

'She is.'

'I'm thrilled. Have you finished?'

'Finished what?'

'Being such a spoilt, manipulative little bitch.'

'I'll be any kind of bitch I want. I *created* you, Polastri. Show some fucking gratitude.'

She's such a jagged cluster of contradictions. I had no idea that anyone could be so ferociously self-sufficient, and at the same time so emotionally unstable. One moment she's flirtatious and tender, covering my face with kisses, the next she's spitting the most wounding things at me that she can think of. I know her cruelty is just a front, a way of protecting her fragile sense of self, but it pierces me like a knife every time. Because right now, if I don't have her I don't have anything. And she knows it.

Perhaps I shouldn't be surprised at Villanelle's behaviour, because although it's crazy to get upset about Rinse-Aid, it makes me realise just how utterly solitary her existence has been. She's never used a dishwasher because she's never

20

needed one: she's always lived and eaten alone. In choosing to save my life, and in doing so risking her own, she went against her own nature.

Why is she doing it? The staging of my death and our escape from London was so bold, so meticulously executed. Why is Villanelle going to so much trouble on my behalf? Does she really care for me, or am I just a fixation, an itch that she has to scratch? And what about me? What do I feel, beyond the fact that I want her, desperately, and live for the moments when we reach for each other in the darkness?

We talk. In fits and starts to begin with, but soon for hours on end. Talking distracts me from the painful stomach contractions I've started experiencing. When they started, like a snake coiling tighter and tighter in my guts, I was afraid I had gastroenteritis or a knotted intestine. I told Villanelle and she laughed, prodded my stomach with a hard finger, and told me I was hungry. 'I had this often when I was a child. It will be bad for a day or two then it will go.'

'And then what?'

'Then your internal organs start to dissolve.'

'Great.'

'I'm kidding. You'll be fine. I knew a fashion model in Paris whose daily diet was a single Ladurée macaroon.'

'Wow. What flavour?'

'*Pistache*.'

'Oh my God. I'd sell my soul for a pistachio macaroon right now.'

'Too late.'

'What do you mean?'

'Your soul's mine now. It's not for sale. You have to starve.'

'Shit. OK, just keep talking.'

'What about?'

'Tell me about Paris.'

'I loved it. I was *une femme mystérieuse*. No one knew who I was, but I'd see people staring at me, and I'd think, fuck, if you only knew. But of course they didn't know. And that felt so good. There was this one guy, very rich . . .'

She always starts by boasting. She loves to describe the revenge that she's visited on those who have underestimated her (a long list), and the ease with which she's outwitted those trying to apprehend her.

Her tendency to fictionalise her life makes it hard to establish a definitive story, but I already know the basic facts, and gradually I fit the pieces together. She was born Oxana Borisovna Vorontsova in Perm, a second-tier industrial city near the Urals. Her mother died of cancer when she was young, her father was a soldier, often absent. Diagnosed with an antisocial personality disorder, Oxana endured a lonely and friendless childhood. She excelled at her studies but was often in trouble for violent and disruptive behaviour. While at secondary school she formed a close attachment to her French teacher, a woman named Anna Leonova. One night, after school, Anna was sexually assaulted at a bus stop. A local youth was suspected of carrying out the attack, and shortly afterwards he was discovered incoherent and suffering from massive blood loss. 'I castrated him,' Villanelle tells me with a touch of smugness. 'I pretended I was going to give him a blow job, then cut off his balls with a knife. No one guessed it was me.'

In fact, the local police had a pretty good idea who was responsible. They already had a juvenile file on Oxana Vorontsova, but abandoned the investigation for lack of evidence. They would be more tenacious when Oxana, by now at university, was arrested for murder. The victims were three local gangsters who, she claimed, had killed her father. This accords with what I was told by Vadim Tikhomirov of the FSB, although Villanelle's version of events differs substantially from the official report. According to her, her father was working undercover for the security services, and had infiltrated the gang. According to the police, he was a low-grade enforcer for the gang and had been caught stealing from his bosses.

While awaiting trial, Oxana's release from prison was engineered by a man named Konstantin. She never knew his full name, but it's probable that this was Konstantin Orlov, a former intelligence officer of considerable distinction and reputation. Orlov had for some years run the FSB's Directorate S, a secretive bureau whose operational remit included the elimination of foreign enemies of the Russian state. By the time that Oxana encountered Orlov, it appears that he was performing a similar service for an organisation called the Twelve. 'He knew everything about me, right back to my childhood,' Villanelle remembers with pride. 'He told me that I had been born to change history.'

What this meant in practical terms was that she became a paid assassin for the Twelve. Orlov supervised her training, and later became her handler, installing her in the apartment in Paris, and at intervals dispatching her on kill missions.

Villanelle loved her new life. The airy apartment over-looking the Bois de Boulogne, the money, the beautiful clothes. She even made a friend, a wealthy young woman named Anne-Laure, with whom she shared lunches at fashionable restaurants, shopping trips, and occasional ménages à trois. I think that what she loved even more than this gilded existence, though, was the secret thrill of knowing that she wasn't the person the world thought she was. When she looked in the mirror, she saw not a chic young socialite, but a dark angel, a bringer of death. She was addicted as much to the secrecy as to the killing itself.

She still is. She doesn't tell me her plans for when we get to Russia because withholding this knowledge gives her power over me. Whether I can persuade her to relax her grip, I don't know. I hope so, because if we can't trust each other we're not going to make it.

I'm not the person I was. The events of the last week have shown me the shadow self I've always denied, and forced me to hear the backbeat I've always pretended wasn't there. All my certainties have evaporated. Villanelle has deleted them.

'Fuck's sake, Villanelle.'
    'What?'
    'You kicked me literally all night.'
    'You farted all night.'
    'I didn't. You're just making that up.'
    'I'm not. It's because you don't shit.'
    'Right, you're a doctor now?'
    'Eve, since we left London you haven't shitted once.'
    'Shat.'

24

'Past tense of shit is shat? You're shitting me.'

'Funny girl. Yes, it's irregular.'

'Like you, *pupsik*. And you know why you haven't shat for a week? Because you're repressed.'

'A psychologist, too. This is fascinating.'

'You're embarrassed. So you hold it in.'

'I do no such fucking thing.'

'You should kill a few people. Get it out of your system. Then you mightn't be so uptight about shitting in front of your girlfriend.'

'Say that again.'

'Say what again?'

'Girlfriend.'

'Girlfriend. Girlfriend, girlfriend, girlfriend. Enough?'

'No. Never stop.'

'You're so whipped.'

'I know. Come here.'

The last night in the container is the worst. The wind screams across our bows, pounding against the container stacks so that they creak and groan. In the darkness, my hunger pangs and the vessel's pitch and roll join forces to nauseating effect. I draw my knees up against my chest and lie open-eyed as acid rises into my throat. Then I'm on my hands and knees, retching uncontrollably, but there's nothing in my stomach to come up. The wind continues its assault for hours, until my body is wrung out and my throat raw from dry heaving.

Throughout it all, Villanelle says not one word, makes not a single sympathetic gesture. A touch would do it, but none is forthcoming. I don't know if she's asleep or awake, angry or indifferent. She's just not there. I feel so utterly abandoned that I half-expect to find myself alone when the morning comes, if it ever comes.

Somehow, I drift off. When I wake an unquantifiable time later the wind has dropped, my stomach cramps have gone, and Villanelle's sleeping body is warm against my back. I lie there unmoving, her arm heavy on mine, her breath whistling across my ear. Careful not to wake her, I manoeuvre myself into a position where I can see my watch. It's gone 6 a.m., Baltic time. Outside the day is dawning, cold and dangerous.

Finally, Villanelle stirs, yawns, stretches like a cat, and buries her face in my hair. 'Are you OK? You sounded awful last night.'

'You were awake? Why didn't you say anything? I thought I was going to die.'

'You weren't going to die, *pupsik*, you were seasick. There was nothing I could say to make you feel better, so I went to sleep.'

'I felt alone.'

'I was right here.'

'Couldn't you have said something?'

'What should I have said?'

'Fuck, I don't know, Villanelle. Just something to tell me that you knew how I was feeling?'

'But I didn't know how you were feeling.' She gets to her feet and stumbles across the clothing bales to the safety hatch. A minute later the interior of the container is illuminated with a thin morning light. Pulling down her leggings and pants, Villanelle squats over the bucket. In her thick sweater she looks shapeless and bedraggled, her hair standing out from her head in spikes. I follow her to the bucket, pee in my turn, then carry it over to the hatch and pour it out. The urine freezes immediately, thickening the cascade of yellowish ice streaking the container's exterior.

Bracing myself against the sub-zero blast of the wind, I search the horizon. Slicing between sea and sky is a faint, grey knife blade. I'm not sure if it's a trick of the light, so I find my glasses in my bike-jacket pocket and look again. It's land. Russia. I stare out of the hatch, trying to focus my thoughts, and then Villanelle is beside me, her cold cheek pressed to mine.

Sniffing, she wipes her nose with her sleeve. 'When we get there, you do exactly what I say, OK?'

'OK.' I watch as the silhouette of St Petersburg slowly hardens. 'Villanelle?'

'Yes.'

'I'm scared. I'm really fucking terrified.'

She slips a hand under my sweater and over my heart. 'It's not a problem. Being scared when you're in danger is normal.'

'Are you scared?'

'No, but I'm not normal. You know that.'

'I do. And I don't want to lose you.'

'You won't lose me, *pupsik*. But you have to trust me.'

I turn to her, and we hold each other, my fingers in her greasy hair, hers in mine. 'It's been a good honeymoon, hasn't it?' she says.

'It's been perfect.'

'You don't mind me being a psychopath?'

I stiffen. 'I've never called you that. Ever.'

'Not to my face.' She bites the lobe of my ear. 'But it's what I am. We both know that.'

I stare out through the safety hatch. Other container vessels are visible now, converging on the distant port.

'Listen, Eve. I know you want me to, you know, try to feel the things that you feel . . .'

Whether it's from hunger, lack of sleep, or just the freezing wind, tears spring to my eyes. 'Sweetie, it's OK, really it is. I . . . I'm happy with how you are.'

'I'll try to be more normal, OK, but if we're going to survive, you're going to have to be a bit more like me. A bit more . . .'

'More Villanelle?'

She brushes my neck with her chapped lips. 'A bit more Oxana.'

# 3

We feel the *Kirovo-Chepetsk* slowing. A glance through the hatch tells us that the approach to St Petersburg is frozen, with the ice extending at least two miles out to sea. For the next few hours we barely move, and then an icebreaker vessel appears off our port bow, and begins cutting a ship lane for us. It's a desperately slow business, and we alternate between lying in frustrated silence on the clothing bales and facing the glacial wind at the hatch as the icebreaker shears, metre by metre, through the creaking, protesting ice.

By the time the *Kirovo-Chepetsk* docks at the terminal in Ugolnaya harbour, and the engine vibrations finally cut out altogether, it's been dark for hours. In the steel box that's been our home for the best part of a week, the air is thick with the smell of our bodies. We've eaten the last of the cheese and chocolate and hunger is tearing at my guts. I'm exhausted, wrung out and terrified, mostly at the thought of being separated from Villanelle. What's her plan? What will happen when the container doors are opened? Where will we be, and what will we face?

Unloading begins a couple of hours after docking. We're one of the first containers to be lifted off the *Kirovo-Chepetsk*, and my heart races as we swing through the air and lock on to the waiting trailer. Zipped into the inside pockets of my motorcycle jacket are the Glock, which presses uncomfortably against my ribs, and three clips of 9mm ammunition. If the container is scanned for body heat, or searched in the course of a security check, God knows what will happen. Igor assured us in Immingham that no such checks would be made, and that our safe transit to a St Petersburg industrial depot would be taken care of, but we are a long way from Immingham now. As the container truck moves off, I reach for Villanelle and touch her cheek. She flinches irritably.

'What?'

'Suppose we're stopped?'

She yawns. 'Fuck's sake, Eve.'

'Well?'

'If we're stopped, just do what I say.'

'You always say that. It doesn't help.'

'I don't give a shit. Stop getting on my tits.'

She turns her back to me, and I lie there, grinding my teeth. Right now I'd welcome arrest if it involved a square meal, and to hell with Villanelle and the future. I imagine a warm office, a steaming bowl of borscht, crusty brown bread, fruit juice, coffee . . . I'm so furious, and so knotted up with hunger and anxiety, that I fail to realise we've left the port area behind us.

The container truck's progress through the outskirts of St Petersburg is unhurried, and we feel every grinding gear change. When we finally come to rest, there's absolute silence. Then a thunderous vibration seizes the container and it tilts sharply, so that everything inside slips downhill and banks up against the rear doors. I go with it, and end up with Villanelle's knee in my face. Hurriedly, arms and legs scrabbling, we drag the bales on top of us. I burrow so far down that I can feel the cold steel floor of the container beneath me. The cargo doors are likely to be opened at any moment, and my heart is beating so violently I'm afraid I'm going to pass out.

With an agonised scraping the container slides to the ground. Minutes pass, and then there's a muted clanking as the locking rods are released and the doors are swung open. Beneath the bales I freeze, my jaw clenched and my eyes squeezed shut, so scared I can't think. The moment stretches out, but I can hear nothing. Vaguely, I become aware of one of Villanelle's arms lying across my back. And then, just metres away, something slams shut, a truck engine grumbles into life, and there's the distant screech of un-oiled gates.

For several minutes, neither of us moves. Then I feel the arm slither away, and the bales shifting. Even so I remain frozen to the container floor, not daring to hope that we're alone. It's only when I hear Villanelle's voice that I open my eyes and glance upwards.

'Hey, dumbass,' she whispers, directing the beam of a red-light torch at my face. 'It's OK. There's no one here.'

'Are you sure?'

'Yes. Come out.'

Hesitantly, I feel my way to the open doors of the container, find my glasses, and look around me. We're in the loading dock of a warehouse the size of a cathedral. Above us, strip lights suspended from rusting joists give off a sick, sulphurous glow. To our left are the dim outlines of the steel doors, now closed, through which the container truck entered and exited. A razor-cut of light shows around a judas gate let into one of the doors. Ahead of us, vanishing into the shadows, stand serried ranks of industrial garment-rails, all holding wedding dresses. It looks like an army of ghostly brides.

Villanelle beckons and I follow. I stop after a few steps, dizzy and light-headed. I feel bloated, and there's a sharp pain lancing through my guts.

'Are you OK?'

I stand there for a moment, swaying. 'Just need to get my balance.'

She frowns, then turns back and jabs a finger into my side. 'Sore?'

'Yes, how did you know?'

'It's obvious. You can't just not shit for a week.'

'I'm sure I'll get round to it soon. Anyway, it's stopped hurting, so let's go.'

We walk the perimeter of the warehouse, but there's no quick way out. There are a couple of steel fire doors, both immovably locked. The windows are way out of reach, at least ten metres from the ground, and the skylight that runs the length of the building is even higher. A small office, accessible by a stairway, is suspended above the shop floor. We climb the stairs. The door is unlocked, and on the desk there are invoices and other documents indicating that the warehouse is owned by a company named Prekrasnaya Nevesta. Beautiful Bride. The desk also holds a cheap TeXet phone and a paper bag containing a stale sausage sandwich.

'Have it,' Villanelle says. 'I'm not hungry.'

She's lying, obviously, but I wolf it down anyway.

'Just don't expect me to kiss you anytime soon,' she says, pulling on a pair of the latex gloves that she always seems to carry around with her. 'That thing stinks. It's probably donkey meat.'

'I won't,' I tell her. 'And I don't care.'

She turns the phone on. It has 1 per cent battery life left. Before it dies in her hands I check the time against my watch. Twenty to six.

'What time do you think people start work here?'

'I saw a punch clock by the entrance. Let's go back down and have a look at the employees' cards.'

It turns out that the first members of the workforce arrive at six, or shortly after. We have barely quarter of an hour. 'When they come in, that's when we need to make our move,' Villanelle says. 'If we try and stay hidden we'll definitely get caught.'

As I search the container, removing the evidence of our stay – rucksacks, empty water bottles, food-wrappings, shit-bags – Villanelle prowls round the warehouse, examining the ranks of wedding dresses. Massive electrical heaters mounted on wheels stand at intervals in the floor's central aisle, and one of these seems to particularly interest her. After a couple of minutes she returns to the container, collects the neatly knotted bags of her own shit, and directs me to a hiding place among the garment rails, about ten or twelve metres from the gate. 'Wait here,' she says, passing me the rucksacks. 'And don't move.'

The minutes pass with agonising slowness. I'm terrified that people will arrive early, Villanelle will be caught out in the open, and I'll be discovered crouching among the wedding dresses. Eventually, however, she reappears beside me. 'When I give the word, run like fuck for the gate,' she tells me, as we put on our rucksacks. 'Don't speak, don't look back, and stay close to me.'

'That's the plan? Run like fuck?'

'That's the plan. Remember, they're civilians. Factory workers. They'll be much more scared of you than you are of them. They won't have any idea what's going on.'

I look at her doubtfully, and at that moment we hear the creak of the judas gate opening. As quickly as I can I take off my glasses and stuff them into a pocket. Then there's a murmur of voices, and an unhurried series of electronic clunks as the Prekrasnaya Nevesta employees begin to punch their timecards. Overhead lights flicker on, there's a whiff of cigarette smoke, and as unseen figures shuffle past our hiding place, the distance between the two of us and the gate seems to grow greater and greater. Cool it, I tell myself, trying to steady my breathing. It'll be like running up Tottenham Court Road for a number 24 bus. Easy-peasy.

A series of vibrant rumblings announces that the heating units have been switched on. Tightening the straps of her backpack, Villanelle moves to a runner's crouch. 'Get ready,' she whispers, and I imitate her, dry-mouthed with apprehension. The rumbling of the heaters becomes a whirr and then there's a spattering sound, ragged screams, an outburst of swearing, and the sound of feet running past us towards the centre of the warehouse. 'Go!' Villanelle mouths, and sprints towards the warehouse entrance, her pack bouncing on her back.

I'm there at her shoulder, running for that bus. Away to our right I'm aware of a confusion of shouting figures and angry faces swivelling towards us. Somehow we reach the judas gate. Villanelle swings it open, we leap through, and race over the rough, frozen ground towards a chain-link fence. Waiting for us at the exit is a security guy in a hi-vis jacket. He stretches out his arms in a tentative attempt to block us and Villanelle whips her Sig Sauer from her jacket and points it at his face. He dives sideways, and I reach past Villanelle for the latch of the exit gate and wrench it open. She pushes through, dragging me after her, but my foot twists on the frozen ground, and I fall heavily onto my hip. I try to stand, but my ankle explodes with pain.

'Get up, Eve,' Villanelle says with quiet urgency, as a shouting mob begins to pour out of the warehouse.

'I can't.'

She looks down at me, her eyes expressionless. 'Sorry, baby,' she says, and runs.

Within moments, I'm surrounded. Everyone's arguing, swearing at me, staring at me, and shouting questions. I curl up in a foetal position on the ground, my knees drawn up to my chest and my eyes closed. I can feel my ankle swelling. It hurts like hell. This is the end.

'*Otkryvay glaza. Vstavay.*' Open your eyes! Stand up! A male voice, harsh and accusatory.

I squint upwards. Angry faces against an iron-grey sky. The speaker is an older man with a shaven head and skull-like features. To his side is a woman, fortyish, with a spectrally pale complexion and discoloured teeth, and a young guy with a spider's-web neck tattoo. Others, perhaps a dozen of them, mill around. They're wearing hoodies, overalls and work boots. Their voices are strident, but most of them just look baffled.

'*Ty kto?*' Who are you?

I don't answer. Perhaps, as Villanelle hoped, they'll think that I'm mentally ill. That I've been driven by voices in my head to commit random acts of trespass and destruction. Perhaps, and this is admittedly a long shot, someone will take me to a hospital, from where I can contact the British authorities. Erratic behaviour as a consequence of post-traumatic stress, I will suggest apologetically, and this will not be far from the truth. I will be flown home and prescribed rest. Niko will take a lot of winning over, but sooner or later he will take me back, and forgive me. And then the Twelve will kill me. Fuck.

'*Ty kto?*'

I stare back at skull-face, and he issues a series of directives. I am yanked to my feet, my rucksack is lifted from my back, and two of the women support me as I half-walk, half-hop back to the warehouse. The young man with the neck tattoo, meanwhile, speaks with quiet urgency into a mobile phone. Now that I'm helpless, and wholly unable to control events, I discover that I'm no longer afraid.

The two women help me over the step and through the judas gate, and I'm immediately assaulted by a stomach-turning stench. It's everywhere, filling my nostrils, throat and lungs, and it gets worse the further we proceed into the building.

'*Zdes vonyayet*,' says one of the women, holding a headscarf over her nose, and I can't help but agree. It stinks.

In front of one of the fan heaters, everything has been sprayed with a fine mist of shit. The floor is slippery with it, as are the ceiling and light fittings, and a dozen of the most elaborate wedding dresses, formerly shell-pink, pearly white or ivory, are unromantically flecked with brown.

Villanelle's improvised diversion has proved shockingly effective. When she was setting it up I was too tense to pay much attention, but I now see what she was up to. Having anticipated that one of the first things that the Prekrasnaya Nevesta workforce would do on arrival at the warehouse was to get the place warmed up, she packed the interior of one of the heating units with a week's worth of her own shit, neatly knotted into six biodegradable bags. The bags would have melted fast, and the fans would have done the rest. The heater in question has been turned off, but it's still steaming and dripping.

Disgusting, but classic Villanelle. A signature piece, you might say, charged with the brilliance and horror that she brings to her finest work. Even as I gag at the stench, I recognise the flair that drew me to pursue her in the first place. I also can't help reading the scene as a personal message. If you're hoping for happy-ever-after, she's saying, then forget it, that's all shit. She clearly meant it, because she's gone. Given the choice between rescuing me and saving herself, she legged it.

Of course she did. She's a psychopath.

The two women lead me to the centre of the warehouse floor, where skullhead is waiting, and a chair has been pulled up for me. My rucksack is placed at my side. All things considered, I'm amazed at their civility and consideration.

'*Ty kto?*' I'm asked again, and again I stare back vacantly.

'*Kto ona takaya?*' Who is she? Skullhead points in the direction that Villanelle went, and I frown as if I don't understand the question, or who he's referring to.

'*Ona bolnaya na golovu,*' says the woman with the head-scarf, and at her suggestion that I have mental health problems I gaze at her piteously and, to my surprise, discover that I'm weeping.

Once I've started, I can't stop. I lean forward in the chair, bury my face in my hands, and sob. I feel my shoulders shake, and the tears run through my fingers. I've lost my husband, my home, and to all intents and purposes, my life. I'm trapped in a country I barely know, forced to use a language I speak poorly, fleeing an enemy I can't begin to identify. Niko thinks I'm dead, but the Twelve will not be so easily deceived. The only person who could have kept me safe was Villanelle, and now I've lost her too.

How long I remain in this self-pitying state, I don't know, but when I finally raise my head, the guy with the neck-tattoo is lowering his phone. 'Dasha Kvariani's coming,' he announces grimly. 'She'll be here any minute.'

Wiping my eyes with the back of my hand, I look at the faces surrounding me. Whoever this Dasha is, her arrival is clearly not good news.

There are five of them. The four men are young, thuggish, and sharply dressed. They stop dead when they enter, pinch their noses, and glance at each other with disbelief. The woman ignores the smell and the milling employees, strides to the centre of the warehouse floor, and looks about her. In these surroundings, she's a vision. Black shearling jacket zipped to the throat, cool green eyes, lustrous chestnut hair cut in a chin-length bob.

She beckons to the men. Two of them approach me, preceded by a dizzying gust of cologne. The first pulls me to my feet and subjects me to a disdainful body search, the second empties my rucksack on the floor and separates the Glock and the ammunition clips from the crumpled sweaters and dirty socks and pants. The woman glances at the handgun. Placing her hands on her knees, she leans forward and stares at me thoughtfully. Then she slaps me, really hard.

I almost fall out of the chair. It's not the stinging force of the blow, it's the assumption that I'm someone who can and should be hit that really shocks me. I gape at her, and she slaps me again. 'So what's your name, you rancid whore?' she asks. Russian insults can be colourful.

Something shifts in me and I remember Villanelle's words. Her demand that I should be more like her. More like Oxana. She wouldn't be slumped in a chair, tearfully waiting for the worst. She'd be ignoring the fear, sucking up the pain, and planning her next move.

I've never hit anyone in my life. So when I propel myself from the chair and punch Dasha Kvariani smack on the tip of her pretty nose, I'm almost as surprised as she is. There's a biscuity crunch, blood jets from her nostrils, and she turns sharply away, clutching her face.

Everyone freezes, and the two men who searched me grab my arms. I'm so high on adrenalin I don't feel a thing. Even my ankle is anaesthetised. The Kvariani woman is swearing vengefully, in a voice thick with blood and mucus. I can't follow all of it, but I catch the words 'ogromnaya blyat *oshibka*', which means 'huge fucking mistake'. She issues a series of orders, and two of the warehouse employees slip away, one returning with a long coil of industrial twine, the other wheeling one of the tall, steel garment hangers.

The two men stand me in front of the hanger and bind my wrists behind my back with the twine, knotting it with practised fingers. My confidence wavers, and I'm not sure that my bad ankle is going to go on supporting me for much longer. As my knees start to shake, the two men lift me by the armpits and stand me on the horizontal bar at the hanger's base, a foot off the ground. Then I feel my wrists wrenched forcefully upwards and suspended from the upper bar. I slump forwards, my arms vertical, pain knifing jaggedly through my neck and shoulders. I fight to retain my balance, knowing that if my feet slip off the bar both of my shoulders will be wrenched out of their sockets, but my knees are gluey and my sprained ankle is on fire.

The pain gets worse, and becomes inseparable from the sound of my gasping and sobbing. Dasha Kvariani steps in front of me, so that all I can see of her is her fur-lined ankle boots. Then a plastic bucket of water is placed beside one of the boots, her hands lift it, and a moment later I'm drenched, and gasping at the icy shock. I jerk and writhe so violently that the garment hanger tips towards the floor. I'm a split second from a smashed face when invisible hands catch the hanger and ease it back upright. There's no feeling in my arms and shoulders now. I have to fight to breathe, dragging the air into my constricted lungs. I'm so cold I can't think.

There's a gunshot, shockingly loud, followed by a dimming of the lights and a pattering of falling glass. Then there's a meaty crack and a thump.

'Dasha Kvariani. You're looking good, *suchka*.' It's Villanelle, her voice deadly calm. I'm so relieved I start to cry. She's come back for me.

'Vorontsova?' Kvariani's voice is thick and unsteady. 'Oxana Vorontsova? I thought you were dead.'

'Wrong. Get her down from there right now, bitch, or you'll be fucking dead.'

Hands untie me, and assist me to a chair. I sit there for a moment, dripping and shaking with cold. Villanelle is standing, legs apart, over the unconscious body of one of the thugs that tied me to the garment rail. He's bleeding from a serious head wound inflicted, I'm guessing, with the butt of Villanelle's Sig Sauer. I'm not sympathetic, and I'm pleased to see that the weapon in question is pointed unwaveringly between Dasha Kvariani's eyes.

'Send someone to get her some dry clothes,' Villanelle orders, glancing at me, and Kvariani gestures to the pale woman, who hurries nervously away, glass from the shot-out ceiling light crunching and snapping beneath her boots.

'Can you please explain to me what the fuck you're doing here?' Kvariani asks Villanelle. 'And put the Sig away. We're both Dobryanka graduates, after all.'

Slowly, Villanelle lowers the gun.

Kvariani points at me. 'Is she yours?'

'Yes.'

'Sorry if we were rough with her. But I have to ask you again, Vorontsova, what the fuck is going on? The owner of this business pays me to make sure there's no trouble here, and I get a call saying that two crazy women have covered the place in human shit, damaged machinery, and destroyed hundreds of thousands of roubles worth of stock. I mean, what am I supposed to do?'

The pale woman returns, and leads me by the hand to a dingy women's toilet. She's found me a T-shirt, a grimy pink sweater, and a faded pair of overalls like those worn by the Prekrasnaya Nevesta employees. A filthy hand-towel hangs on the back of the door. Gesturing vaguely at the clothes, the woman disappears. By the time I've changed into the dry clothing and limped back to the others, Villanelle and Dasha Kvariani are talking and laughing together. Where the thug with the head wound was lying is now just a long blood-smear. At my approach Villanelle and Dasha look up.

'You look cute,' Villanelle tells me in English. 'Proletarian chic suits you.'

'Yeah, very funny. You did notice, just five minutes ago, that your new best friend was torturing me?'

'Hey, she apologises, she's really sorry about that. And she's an old friend, not a new one. We know each other from prison.'

'Small world.'

'Yeah, well. Dasha was famous in Dobryanka, everyone called her "Necksnapper". Her father was a respected gang leader in the *vorovskoy mir*. He was so powerful in St Petersburg the prosecutors didn't dare try Dasha in a local court, they sent her fifteen hundred kilometres away to Perm. And her family still managed to fix everything.'

'Great.'

'*Anglichanka?*' asks Dasha, flashing her teeth at me. 'You're English?'

I ignore her. My shoulder muscles are still agony. 'So why was she on trial?' I ask Villanelle in English. 'What did she do?'

'She was on the Metro one evening, going home from college. The train was like super-crowded, and some guy started feeling her up.'

'On my bum,' says Dasha. 'So I . . .' She mimes taking the guy's head in her arms and violently twisting it. 'His neck maked sound like . . . *popkorn.*'

'Jesus.'

'I know, right?'

'Weren't there witnesses?'

'Yes, but my father speaked with them.' She switches to Russian.

'She says it was her Me Too moment,' Villanelle explains.

# 4

'I guess you should start calling me Oxana,' she says, a little regretfully.

'I guess I should. I liked Villanelle.'

'I know. Cool name. But too dangerous to use now.'

'Mmm. OK . . . Oxana.'

We're lying at opposite ends of a huge old enamel bath in Dasha's apartment. Tall windows overlook a broad highway from which the rumble and hiss of traffic and the clanking of trams are dimly audible. Oxana, needless to say, has taken the end of the bath without the taps, but the hot water is bliss after our confinement in the container.

The apartment is on the third floor of a massive neoclassical block in an area called Avtovo. The building must once have been very grand, the sort of property where senior Communist Party officials and their families lived, but it has clearly been in decline for decades. The fittings are worn, the lift creaks, the plumbing clanks and grumbles.

'Look at the colour of this bath water,' Oxana says, playing with my toes.

'I know, gross. And you farting all the time doesn't help.'

'It does help. It's fun. Watch. Squeeze asshole, little bubbles. Relax asshole, bigger bubbles.'

'Awesome.'

'When you live alone, you get good at stuff like this.'

'I'm sure. So what's the deal with Dasha?'

'How do you mean, what's the deal?'

'I mean are we her guests, her prisoners . . .?'

'Dasha and I were in Dobryanka prison together, and under the criminal code, the *vorovskoy zakon*, we are sisters. Murder sisters. That means that she has to help me. I told her I was a *torpedo*, a shooter, for a powerful family in Europe, and that I had to get out fast. She doesn't need to know more than that at this stage.'

'And me?'

'She didn't ask about you.'

'I'm just the *torpedo*'s girlfriend?'

'You want me to say you worked for MI6? Seriously? I told her what I had to tell her to get her trust, because right now, we need her. We need new identities, new passports, all that shit, and she can fix it. Or at least she's connected to people who can fix that. Basically, we can stay here as long as we need to, she'll help us, and she won't give us up. But she'll also expect me to do something for her in return. Something big. So we have to wait and see what that something turns out to be.'

'So what am I supposed to do?'

'Nothing. Can we have some more hot water? It's getting cold at this end.'

'There isn't any more hot water. What do you mean, nothing?'

'I mean you just, I don't know, hang out or whatever. Dasha knows you're my woman. She won't involve you in any criminal stuff.'

'Wow. That sounds . . . Fuck, I don't know what it sounds like.'

She takes an experimental bite of my big toe. 'You want to be a gangster, *pupsik*?'

'I want to be by your side. I didn't come all this way just to go shopping.'

'I did. I'm going to make you look so amazing.'

'I'm serious, Oxana. I'm not just your babe.'

'Yes, you are. You know your feet taste of Emmental cheese? The sort with the big holes in?'

'You are seriously fucking weird, you know that?'

'I'm weird? You're the one in the bath with the psychopath.'

I try to get my head comfortable against the taps. 'What sort of criminal stuff is Dasha into?'

'The usual. Smuggling, credit cards, protection, drugs . . . Probably mostly drugs. Her father Gennadi led a brigade for the Kupchino Bratva, which controls the St Petersburg heroin trade, and when he retired he passed the leadership of the brigade to Dasha. It's almost unknown for a woman to hold rank in the gangs, but she was already a fully initiated *vor*, and people respected her.'

'I bet. She's a fucking sadist.'

'Eve, *pupsik*, you have to move on from this morning. See it from her point of view. That Prekrasnaya Nevesta warehouse pays her to protect them, and we did make quite a mess in there. Dasha had to be seen to be taking control of the situation.'

'She didn't have to torture me.'

'She only tortured you a bit.'

'She'd have tortured me a lot if you hadn't turned up.'

'She was just doing her job. Why is it that when a woman is assertive in the workplace she's always seen as a bitch?'

'Huge question.'

'I'll tell you. It's because we expect men to torture and kill people, but when women do it it's seen as violating gender stereotypes. It's ridiculous.'

'I know, sweetie, life's unfair.'

'It really is. And just for your information' – she kicks bathwater in my face – 'I'd appreciate a thank-you for rescuing you this morning.'

'Thank you to my protective, feminist girlfriend.'

'You're so full of shit.'

Dasha, I have to admit, takes very good care of us. The apartment is impersonal, and the room she assigns to us has an unaired, unused feel to it. The windows, which are locked shut, have the thick, greenish look of bulletproof glass. But the bed is comfortable enough, and after breakfast, which is brought to us by a young woman who introduces herself as Kristina, we both fall fast asleep again.

When we wake it's almost midday, and we're ravenous again. The apartment appears to be empty except for Kristina, who has clearly been waiting for us to surface. Handing us each a warm down-filled jacket, she leads us out of the flat, and we descend to the street in the shuddering lift. My ankle is less swollen than it was, and although it's still sore, I can walk.

It's good to be in direct sunlight. The sky is dark azure blue, and the morning's snowfall has frozen, dusting the grimy, yellow-brown buildings with sparkling white. Lunch is a Big Mac and fries, and then Kristina walks us a short distance down Stachek Prospekt to a second-hand store in a converted cinema, the Kometa. The seats have been removed from the auditorium, which now holds rank after rank of clothing stalls. These offer everything from goth and punk fashions to old theatre costumes, military and police regalia, fetish-wear and home-made jewellery. The place smells musty and cloying, as such places always do, and it's oddly poignant to wander down the aisles beneath the art deco chandeliers, picking through the tattered residue of other people's lives.

'In these clothes, you'll look as if you've lived in St Petersburg for ever, like subculture people,' Kristina says. Tall and long-legged, with hair the colour of wheat and a gentle, hesitant manner, she's an unlikely member of a gangster household. She doesn't speak often, and when she does it's so quietly that we strain to hear her.

Oxana gives my waist a squeeze. 'Reinvent yourself, *pupsik*. Go crazy.'

In this spirit, I make a point of choosing things I'd never have considered in my former life. A midnight-blue velvet coat, its silk lining in tatters, its label identifying it as the property of the Mikhailovsky Theatre. A studded jacket painted with anarchist slogans. A mohair sweater striped in black and yellow like a bee. It occurs to me that I'm enjoying myself, something I've never felt while buying clothes before. Oxana seems to be having a pretty good time too. She's as ruthless out shopping as she is in every other area of her life, not hesitating to rip a garment out of my hands if she wants it for herself.

A visit to a nearby hairdressing and nail salon completes our makeover. Kristina pays for everything from a large roll of cash, which I'm guessing is Dasha's. In the salon she sits quietly, staring into space, as Oxana and I are attended to. The stylist gives me a short, choppy bob, while Oxana gets a spiky pixie cut. My nails end up turquoise, hers black. When we're done Kristina gives us a rare, shy smile. 'Now you look like proper Russians,' she tells us.

Afterwards, we take a taxi to Aviatorov Park. Why Kristina wants to take us there, I'm not sure. Maybe it's the nearest thing to a tourist attraction that Avtovo has to offer. As the sky darkens, and flurries of new snow whirl around us, we mooch across the near-deserted park to a frozen lake girded by dark, skeletal trees. On the far shore, a Soviet monument stands on a promontory. A MiG fighter aircraft leaping into the sky, arrested at the moment of take-off. Kristina indicates it perfunctorily before continuing on her ghostly way along the icy lakeside path. Only then does it occur to me that she has been ordered to keep us away from the apartment for as long as possible, so that Dasha can search our possessions and decide what to do about us. Which might include selling us out.

I ask Oxana about this, and she's doubtful. 'The only people who'd be interested in me, in us, are the Twelve, and they operate at a much higher level than outfits like the Kupchino Bratva.'

'Dasha might have heard of them, though. Presumably she has access to all kinds of underworld information sources.'

'I'm sure she has, but they wouldn't lead her to the Twelve.'

'Supposing she did make the connection. Just for the sake of argument.'

'How would she get in touch with them? On Facebook?'
I nod, not quite convinced.

'Look, Dasha didn't get to be a brigadier in a *bratva* by
being stupid. If she breaks the *vory* code and betrays me to
the Twelve or anyone else, she won't ever be trusted again.
Also, I'd kill her. Maybe not immediately, but one day I'd
come for her, and she knows it.'

Days pass, and I begin to feel stronger. My shoulders are
still painful, especially in the mornings, and I can't walk far
without my ankle protesting. But Dasha feeds us well, and
the effects of living in a container on starvation rations are
beginning to ebb. Oxana runs every day, sometimes for two
or three hours, and pushes herself through a rigorous exercise routine on her return. I spend the time trying to improve
my Russian by reading Dasha's back issues of *Vogue* and
listening to Radio Zenith, the local current affairs channel.

Sleeping with Oxana is so different from sleeping with
Niko. Where Niko's body was unambiguous, so familiar
that it was part of my waking and sleeping, Oxana's body
is enigmatic. The more I explore it, the more mysterious it
seems. Hard and soft, yielding and predatory. She draws me
deeper and deeper. There are times when she slides into an
impenetrable silence, or pushes me away from her, tense
with anger at some imagined slight, but mostly she's skit-
tish and tender. She's like a cat, yawning and stretching and
purring, all lean muscle and sheathed claws. When we sleep,
she faces outwards and I fold into her. She snores.

She keeps the details about our departure from England
vague, and is confident that Dasha believes her, more or
less. She's asked Dasha about fixing us up with Russian

interior passports and new identities. This appears to be possible, for a price.

What Oxana hasn't yet raised with Dasha is the question of Lara Farmanyants, currently languishing in Butyrka jail in Moscow. Personally, I'd be happy to see the bitch rot there for ever. Not only is she Oxana's ex, she also tried to kill me. But Oxana wants her out of there, and is planning to ask Dasha whether it might be possible, through her *vory* connections, to make this happen.

I try not to let the idea of Lara upset me, but Oxana knows how vulnerable I feel when compared to her former girlfriend, and misses no opportunity to drop references to Lara's amazing physique, athleticism and sexual virtuosity. There's a rational part of me that knows that she can't possibly miss Lara in the way that she claims to, and probably doesn't give her a moment's thought from one day to the next. But love is not rational, and for all Oxana's casual cruelties, I have stopped pretending to myself that I'm not in love with her.

I know that I can never tell her this, just as I'm certain that she will never tell me that she loves me, because those words have no meaning for her. I know that I have only myself to blame. I believed that I could somehow finesse her affectless nature, and in the cold light of day I see this to be impossible. St Petersburg winter days are short, however, and the nights are long. In our shared bed, wrapped in darkness and dreams and the warm smell of her body, I find myself believing it again.

A week after our arrival, Kristina directs Oxana and me to a department store where there is a photo booth. When we return, Dasha takes the prints and tells us that we should have our Russian internal passports and other identity documents within the week. In total, for both of us, the cost will be fifteen hundred US dollars, which Oxana pays immediately. There are cheaper versions available, Dasha says, but they are recognisable as forgeries. I'm glad to see the money handed over, because I'm beginning to feel uncomfortable about accepting Dasha's hospitality on an indefinite basis, *vory* code or no *vory* code. I'm also aware of Oxana's increasing restlessness, which running and exercise cannot assuage. 'I need to work,' she tells me, pacing the flat like a caged panther. 'I need to feel I'm alive.'

'Don't I make you feel alive?' I ask, and immediately wish that I hadn't. Oxana turns a pitying gaze on me and says nothing.

After pocketing the cash for the documents, Dasha informs us that she's hosting a dinner at the apartment that evening. Her boss is coming, his name is Asmat Dzabrati, and we should address him as *Pakhan*, or leader. He is a hugely respected figure, apparently. A gangster boss of the old school, who in his younger days was known for dispatching rivals with an axe. With the Pakhan will be the gang's three other brigadiers, Dasha herself being the fourth. It's an important occasion, Dasha impresses on us, and she's anxious for it to go well. Kristina will lend us the appropriate clothes.

Oxana is in a vile mood, so the session doesn't go well. She glances into Kristina's wardrobe, snatches a Saint Laurent tuxedo suit, holds it against herself, glances in the mirror and walks out without a word.

Kristina watches her go. 'Everything OK?'

'Oh . . . you know.'

She smiles faintly. 'I do know.'

'Kristina?'

'Kris.'

'Kris . . . are you with Dasha?'

'Yes. For a year now.'

I stare at the array of dresses, not knowing where to start. 'Do you love her?' I ask impulsively.

'Yes, and she loves me. One day we're going to move out of the city to a village in Karelia. Maybe adopt a daughter.'

'Good luck with that.'

She takes a ruffled silk Bora Aksu dress from the rail, looks at it, and frowns. 'You and your Oxana. You're going to live happily ever after, is that the plan?'

'Something like that.'

She hands me the dress. 'She's a killer, isn't she? A professional.'

I hold her gaze. Listen to the sound of my own breathing.

'I can recognise them straight away. That look they have. Do you like the name Elvira? I think it's so pretty for a little girl.'

Asmat Dzabrati is one of the least remarkable men I've ever met. Short, with thinning hair and mild, rabbity eyes, he's the last of the evening's guests to arrive. His entrance is low-key, but he's immediately the centre of attention. The Pakhan wields the kind of power that doesn't proclaim itself, but is evident in the demeanour of others. As he is helped from his shabby overcoat, led to a chair, and furnished with a drink, the other guests enact an elaborately deferential dance, positioning themselves around him in hierarchical ranks. The inner circle consists of Dasha and the other brigadiers, then there's a cordon of bodyguards and foot soldiers, and finally the wives and girlfriends. Oxana threads herself between these groups like a shark, never quite finding a resting place, while I drift around the outer perimeter of scented, dressed-to-kill women, smilingly listening in on conversations, and moving on if there's any suggestion that I'm expected to do more than nod in agreement.

We're in the apartment's principal reception room. This is furnished with heavy grandeur and dominated by a spot-lit portrait of Dasha lounging in a smoking jacket, holding a cigar. Opposite the painting, between the tall windows overlooking Stachek Prospekt, an ice-sculpture of the Russian president riding a bear drips on a sideboard. At the far end of the room a white-jacketed steward with a bandaged head is serving drinks at a generously stocked bar. Belatedly, I recognise the gang member that Oxana laid out cold in the warehouse. His colleagues mock him, slapping him condescendingly on the cheek as they collect their drinks, laughing at his idiocy in allowing himself to be hospitalised by a woman.

I take a glass of pink Latvian champagne from the bandaged barman, who eyes me ruefully, and search the crowd for Oxana. She's deep in conversation with Dasha, and although I can't hear what either of them is saying I can see the sly flash of Oxana's eyes and Dasha's slow, complicit smile. They look at me and laugh, and although I'm tempted to hurl my glass at them, I sip the sweet, ice-cold champagne instead.

Kris materialises beside me. She looks elegant in grey chiffon, but out of place among the glittering Kupchino Bratva women, like a moth among fireflies. 'They're so boring,' she murmurs to me. 'It's impossible to have an intelligent conversation with any of them. They only talk about three things. Clothes, kids, and how to stop their men screwing around.'

'Oh, God.'

'Exactly. Oh God! They're endlessly telling me how the nanny's so lazy, how she spends her whole time stuffing herself from the fridge and WhatsApping her friends and ignoring little Dima or Nastya, and then they look at me pityingly, like they've just remembered, and say, "But of course, you haven't got children, have you? Do you think you might have some if you met the right guy?" And of course I have to be polite and play along, because Dasha would be high-key angry if I was rude to them, but I want to say, "You know what, bitches? There's never going to be a 'right guy', so suck on that."'

For Kris, this is quite a speech.

'Are you sure this whole *vorovskoy mir* is for you?' I ask her.

She gives me a weary smile. 'I love Dasha, and this is her world, so I guess it has to be for me. How did you and Oxana meet?'

I'm wary. Has Dasha instructed her to fish for information about us? But then I drain my champagne glass and look Kristina in the eye, and she's so transparently guileless, and I so badly need an ally, that I'm almost tempted to tell her the truth.

I don't, though.

Clapping her hands to announce that dinner is served, Dasha squires the Pakhan out of the room. The rest of us follow the two of them at a sedate pace into an ornate dining room, where a long table has been set for twenty. A crystal chandelier sends out rainbow spikes of light, the air is heavy with the scent of lilies, and along the centre of the table, framed by gold cutlery and glassware, a glazed sturgeon is laid out like a corpse. Place cards indicate where we should sit and the protocol is strict. The Pakhan occupies the place of honour, flanked by Dasha and another brigadier, the soldiers are arranged on either side of them, and the women cluster around the table-ends.

Oxana, looking fabulous in the tuxedo suit, has been placed between two of the soldiers, and I watch as her eyes narrow with anger as she realises that she has not been seated among the Kupchino Bratva elite. I've learnt the hard way just how badly she reacts to any perceived disrespect. Something flips in her. Possessed by the need to reassert control over the situation, she's capable of the most lacerating viciousness. I watch as one of the men tries to converse with her and is icily ignored. I could have told him not to bother. When she's like this she's impossible.

'So which is your man?' asks the woman seated on my left, as a selection of blinis, salads and caviar is brought to the table, along with silver trays of vodka in shot glasses. A glance at her place card tells me that her name is Angelina. She has nervous eyes and hair the colour of burnt caramel.

'I'm with Oxana,' I tell her. 'Over there, in the black suit.'

She regards me uncertainly for a moment. 'Pavel,' she says, nodding to one of the men whom Oxana is studiously

57

ignoring. 'My husband. He's a *boyevik*. One of Dasha's crew.'

'So how does he feel about working for a woman?'

'He says he doesn't mind, because she's clever like a man.'

'So what do you do?' I ask, piling caviar onto a blini.

'What do you mean, do?'

'Like do you work, or . . .?'

'I put up with Pavel and all his bullshit precisely so I don't have to work.' She glances downwards at her cleavage, which has been sprinkled with tiny gold stars. 'That's why we're married to these *bratva* guys. They're wealthy. Not Forbes Rich List wealthy but, you know, comfortable. So where do you come from? Your Russian is like, really weird.'

'I'm from London. It's a long story.'

'And this Oxana, you're friends, or . . .'

'Partners.'

'Business partners?'

'Life partners.'

Her face goes blank for a moment, then she brightens. 'That's a really beautiful dress, where did you buy it?'

I'm saved from answering by Dasha, who stands, raises her glass, and proposes an elaborate toast to the Pakhan. 'Long life and good health to the father of our *bratva*,' she concludes. 'Death to our enemies. Strength and honour to our fatherland.'

The Pakhan blinks, smiles his rabbity smile, and touches his shot glass to his lips.

'I'd also like to welcome my sister Oxana,' Dasha continues. 'We holidayed together in Dobryanka, the finest resort in the Urals. And believe me, friends, she was one tough bitch. They told us that she'd hanged herself in her cell, but here she is, alive and well.'

Oxana bows, grins, and raises her glass to Dasha. 'From one tough bitch to another, *spasibo*.'

At this point Dasha evidently thinks she should bring me into the conversation. 'You and Oxana had quite a journey, didn't you? The Baltic container route can be quite cold, I believe?'

A polite silence descends on the table, and nineteen faces turn towards me. I force a smile and, suddenly unconfident of my Russian, attempt to explain that Oxana and I spent the entire week shivering.

Dasha's eyes widen with shock, and she starts to laugh. Everyone else joins in, even the Pakhan. The men stare at me and at each other, spluttering as they repeat my words, and Dasha has tears running down her cheeks. The laughter goes on and on, as I look desperately from face to face. Even Kris is smiling. 'Don't worry,' one of the brigadiers says, wiping his eyes with his napkin. 'You're among friends. Your secret's safe with us.' Only one person is not amused, and that is Oxana, who is staring at me with icy, undiluted hatred.

The meal seems to go on for ever. Endless courses of soup, baked meat, ash-roasted beetroot, sturgeon with porcini mushrooms, dumplings and pastries. And vodka, glass after tiny glass of it. Citrus vodka, cardamom vodka, raspberry, pepper and bison grass vodka. Every couple of minutes someone proposes a toast. To companionship, loyalty, honour, the *vory* life, beautiful women, absent friends and death. I try to sip discreetly rather than swig, but am soon hopelessly, wretchedly, drunk. Time slows to a ticking standstill. The conversation and laughter rise and fall, the room swims in and out of focus. Angelina and others attempt conversation, but give up when they discover that I can only manage slurred and simplistic responses. From time to time I glance over at Oxana, but she is making a point of avoiding my gaze, and conversing animatedly and flirtatiously with everyone around her. The briefest complicit smile or sympathetic glance would turn the evening around for me, but none is forthcoming. Instead, her eyes slide over me as if I'm simply not there.

Finally, mercifully, the last toast has been drunk. *Na pososhok*, one for the road. Everyone stands, and the Pakhan is escorted from the dining room by his bodyguards. Standing at the door, I watch the guests file past. Some smile at me, some shake hands; one or two of the women, clearly as drunk as I am, embrace me like old friends. As Oxana passes, her face is stone.

The apartment empties, leaving Dasha, Kris and Oxana standing in front of the glassy remains of the ice sculpture. 'Go to bed,' Oxana orders me as I approach. 'Dasha and I need to talk.'

'Planning another torture session?' I ask, and Dasha has the grace to look uncomfortable. 'Can I just say I've had the loveliest evening. The food was divine and your friends are delightful. I particularly liked the Pakhan. He's a riot.'

'Eve, please,' Oxana murmurs. 'Haven't you embarrassed yourself enough tonight? Do us all a favour and fuck off.'

I obey, picking my way carefully through the thick silence to our bedroom. There, I sit on the edge of the bed for ten

60

minutes, listening to the thudding of my pulse as the vodka creeps through my system. Drawing back a curtain, I watch as a tram rumbles laboriously down the street, sparks intermittently cascading from its overhead cable. Then I go to the chest of drawers, open the second drawer, and take the Glock from beneath my bee-striped sweater. I'm sorry that I haven't yet had the chance to wear the sweater, but it's time to face the fact that my life is over. I have made a catastrophic series of decisions, the worst of which was entrusting my life to a murderer with mental health issues whose interest in me was fleeting at best. She persuaded me that there was nowhere else to hide, that she was my only chance of survival, and I in my turn persuaded myself that this was true.

Pathetic really, but it no longer matters. I've burnt my bridges. I'm stateless, loveless and alone.

When I shoot myself, will it hurt? Will my last sensation be one of unimaginable pain? Or is it as they say, that you don't hear the shot that kills you, let alone feel it. That it's just . . . lights out?

I don't think I can bear the idea of a head shot. I don't want to be found with half my skull missing and my brains all over the silk-upholstered headboard and the damask curtains. I don't particularly like Dasha, but neither do I want to force her to redecorate.

A heart shot, then. That will be appropriate in so many ways. It'll probably take me a few moments longer to die, but I won't be disfigured. Taking off my glasses, I put them on the bedside table. Then I kick off my shoes, and lie down on the bed with two pillows supporting my upper body. Here we go. An end to fear, to worry, to everything.

When I'm comfortable on the pillows, I slap the maga-zine into the Glock and rack the slide. The gun is now cocked, but to shoot myself in the heart I have to invert it, place the barrel against my chest, and slip the pad of my thumb through the trigger guard. This is an awkward manoeuvre when you're drunk. Glocks don't have a safety catch, they have a double trigger. You have to engage both parts, and I'm just aligning them with my thumb when a faint sound penetrates my consciousness.

It's Oxana. One moment she's standing by the door, the next she's on top of me, wrenching the Glock from my hands. I stare up at her. She's shouting, but the move-ment of her mouth doesn't correspond to the words. She bounces off the bed, stalks over to the window, wrenches open the curtains, and stands with her back to me. There's a metallic rasp and snap as she makes the Glock safe.

'What did you think you were doing?' Her voice is low, barely audible.

'What did it look like?'

'You're not that stupid.'

'It wouldn't be stupid. Give me one fucking reason to carry on.'

She frowns. 'Us.'

'Us? Oxana, I just make you angry. You don't tell me your plans, and when you speak to me, it's like you hate me. There is no us.'

'Eve, please.'

'That's what I mean. That tone of voice. I annoy you.'

'So you decide to kill yourself?'

'Have you got a better idea?'

She walks back to the bed. 'You are such a dumbass, Eve. Such a fucking dumbass.'

'Actually, I'm not. I'm pretty smart. The dumbass is you.'

She sits on the bed, reaches out a hand, and touches my cheek. I slap her hand away, swing my legs over the side of the bed and sit bolt upright, shaking with fury.

'You look very sexy in that dress.'

I ignore her, stand up, and start to walk towards the door, although I have no real idea where I'm going. She jumps off the other side of the bed, bounds across the room, and blocks my path. I don't slow down, but throw out an arm in front of me, grab her by the throat, and slam her hard against the wall. I hold her there, she gasps and her eyes widen, but she doesn't resist.

'I want you to show me some kindness,' I tell her, spitting the words in her face. 'I don't give a shit if that's hard for you. It's time you learnt how to be a fucking human being.'

'I see.' Behind my hand, her neck is throbbing like an anaconda.

'No, you don't see, because you're too fucking lazy to see. You hide behind your psycho label because it gets you off the hook. But you're not just some walking mental health disorder, and you know it.'

'So what am I?' she sneers. 'When you've finished choking me. Which I'm enjoying, by the way.'

'Someone who can't deal with the fact that you have, within your reach, a real living, breathing person who has given up everything for you. Everything.'

Almost casually, Oxana drives her knuckles into my extended elbow, so that the nerve-shock jolts to my fingertips. I release her neck. Then she grabs one of my ears and a hank of my hair in each of her hands. and pulls my face to hers, so that we're eye to eye, nose to nose, mouth to mouth. 'So what do you want in return, Eve?' she whispers.

In response, I take her lower lip between my teeth, and bite it. Oxana exhales softly, and I taste her blood. 'I want you,' I tell her. 'I want to be yours, and I want you to be mine.'

We stand there for a moment, neither of us moving, just breathing.

'All the way?' she asks.

'All the way.'

She pulls her head back so that she can look at me, and slowly traces my face with her forefinger. Across my eyebrow, down my cheekbone, and between my lips, which are glued together with her blood. It dries fast.

'OK,' she says. 'OK.' Taking my glasses from the bedside table, she fits them carefully over my face. 'There, now you can see me properly.'

'You're still a bitch,' I whisper, taking her hands in mine.

'I know, *pupsik*. I'm sorry.' She looks at me gravely. 'Tomorrow, we sit down and plan. Together. Dasha is getting us passports and money, but I have to do something for her. *We* have to do something for her.'

'What's that?'

'Can we talk about it tomorrow?' She pulls me towards her. 'Because right now I have other things in mind.'

'Really? What sort of things?'

'Just . . . things.'

'I'm quite drunk.'

'I noticed. Me too. But not that drunk.'

*

An hour later, I'm almost asleep when a thought occurs to me. 'Sweetie?'

'Mmm?'

'Why did everyone laugh at me at dinner? When I said that I spent the whole week shivering. What was so funny? They all, like, pissed themselves.'

'It was your Russian. Shivering is *drozhala*, and you said *drochila*.'

'What does *drochila* mean?'

'Masturbating.'


'Sweetie?'

'Eve please, shut the fuck up and let me sleep.'

'What did Dasha ask you to do?'

'You really need to know right this second?'

'I really do.'

'She asked me to kill the Pakhan.'

# 5

The next fortnight passes swiftly, and for the first time since we left London, Oxana seems calm and focused. She's naturally secretive, an archetypal lone wolf, and planning an assassination with me is not easy for her. It isn't easy for me, either; murder is murder after all, even if the intended victim is a horrible person like the Pakhan. But we've both kept going. Oxana has begun to share her thoughts with me, and I've managed to ignore what she dismissively refers to as my 'civilian guilt', and concentrate on practicalities and logistics. I've always been good at that.

I'm touched by how hard she's trying to make our collaboration work, and more than that, to make our relationship work. She has no instinct directing her here. She knows how to excite, manipulate and hurt me, but despite the fact that we've lived in each other's pockets for the best part of a month, she still finds my feelings impossible to read. I catch her sometimes, gazing at me with her sea-grey eyes, trying to access my emotions. I find this so heart-rending. I can't imagine how lonely it must be to have your nose forever pressed against the glass separating you from other people. To be eternally out in the cold, trying to look in.

I'll make her feel my love, even if it kills me.

Asmat Dzabrati, the Pakhan, is sixty-nine years old. He lives in an apartment in a massive, grey seventeen-storey building on Malaya Balkanskaya Ulitsa, near Kupchino Metro station. He owns several apartments there, which are occupied by, among others, his four bodyguards, his ex-wife Yelena, and his sister Rushana and her husband. He also leases a small apartment behind the Fruzensky department store, a short drive away, where he keeps his 'sugar baby', a twenty-four-year-old Ukrainian woman named Zoya whom he met through an introduction agency. His family and Yelena disapprove of this relationship, and refuse to acknowledge Zoya, so she never visits the Malaya Balkanskaya building.

The Pakhan's regular ports of call are Zoya's apartment, a clinic in Nevsky Prospekt where Zoya goes for Botox shots and he for rejuvenation injections, and the Elizarova bathhouse in Proletarskaya. Meetings with the Kupchino Bratva brigadiers are either conducted at an Ossetian restaurant named Zarina, where a private room is reserved for the Pakhan and his guests, or at the bathhouse. Occasionally Dzabrati also entertains at home, with Rushana acting as hostess to gang members and their families. At intervals he visits his cardiologist at a private clinic in the city centre. He has a heart condition, believed to be atrial fibrillation, for which he takes Digoxin tablets.

This information has been provided by Dasha, and has been confirmed by surveillance operations mounted by

Oxana. I've been involved in some of these, but always at a distance. Mostly I remain by myself in the apartment on Stachek Prospekt, collating and processing information. I'd like to be out there with Oxana, but she's afraid I would get lost or attract attention in some way. She's probably right. I have a terrible sense of direction, and when I was sent on a course with A4, MI5's watcher department, I struggled embarrassingly, and could never get the communications protocol right.

So Oxana goes alone, which is how she prefers it. On a couple of occasions she's disappeared for over twenty-four hours at a stretch, returning cold, hungry and dog-tired. At these times I know better than to even try to talk to her. Instead I run her a bath, bring her cheese and cucumber sandwiches and cups of tea, and put her to bed.

All the intelligence we acquire goes into a file, which we scour continuously for recurring patterns. So far we've found none. For all his old-school leadership style, the Pakhan is wary as a fox, and according to Oxana well versed in counter-surveillance. Arrangements and appointments are invariably made at the last minute, decoy cars are used, and his drivers always vary the routes that he travels. As far as we can discover he never uses public transport.

We're looking for cracks in this facade. Vulnerabilities that we can exploit. I've decided to think of the operation as an intellectual exercise, rather as I used to view my activities at MI5. When I found myself in pursuit of Oxana I lost this sense of distance and became over-involved. With this project I'm determined to re-find my objectivity.

*

'Why don't you have a bath?' I ask Oxana. 'I'll run one. We can get in together.'

'Not until I've figured this out.'

'Not until *we've* figured it out.'

'Whatever.'

We're in our bedroom, sitting in dusty velveteen armchairs, working through murder scenarios. Oxana's reaction to problem-solving seems to be to suspend all activity relating to hygiene, and she's looking particularly grungy this morning. Her hair is standing out from her head in a crown of greasy spikes, her jeans are in shreds, and the grimy pink sweater from the Prekrasnaya Nevesta warehouse, which she has stolen from me and worn every day for a week, is giving off a deathly smell.

'Has Dasha told you exactly why she wants the Pakhan eliminated?' I ask Oxana.

'She doesn't need to.'

'She wants to run the *bratva*?'

'She sees that he's weakening. Getting older, losing his grip. So she has to make her move, because if she doesn't, one of the others will. It's just how it works.'

'And then what happens?'

'As soon as the Pakhan is dead, Dasha calls a meeting of the other brigadiers and announces that she's in charge. No one will say out loud that she was responsible for killing him, but everyone will know it, and they'll also know that if they give her any shit they'll be taken out too.'

'Will it be a problem that she's a woman?'

'It shouldn't be, but it will be. Women are very poorly

represented in the field of Russian organised crime. Dasha told me the statistics and they're horrifying.'

'So we're—'

'Yes, *pupsik*, we're doing a good thing here.'

I'm not convinced. But here we are. As Oxana says, if we don't take Dzabrati out, someone else will. So we might as well accept the contract, get our papers and money, and disappear. I'm concerned that if we stay here too long, word of us will somehow get back to the Twelve.

'Let's review our options,' I suggest. 'Are we sure we can't get into his building?'

'We could, but it would be difficult. These big Soviet apartment blocks with the narrow corridors were designed for easy surveillance of everyone coming and going. There are two elevators serving the building, both very slow, and there's always one *boyevik* at the street entrance and another on the ninth floor, where the Pakhan and his people live. Also, Dzabrati is never alone in his apartment. There's always a bodyguard. Add in family members, kids . . . It's not impossible, nothing's impossible, but there have got to be easier options.'

'OK. Zoya's place.'

'Possible. He's driven there two or three times a week, usually in the late evening. A bodyguard takes him up to Zoya's apartment, waits outside while he does whatever he does to her, and then walks him back to the car.'

'That's so disgusting. He's what? Forty-five years older than her?'

'Poverty's disgusting, Eve. Believe me, I've been there. As well as the flat she probably gets a generous allowance, like thousands of dollars a month, and instead of working as a cleaner or a cam-girl in some shithole in Ukraine, she gets to spend her day getting beauty treatments and buying nice clothes.'

'Yeah. Except that she has to be available to creepy old rabbit-face whenever he feels like sex. And I truly hate to think what kind of sex he likes.'

'I doubt he's up to anything too heavy. He's got that heart thing, and if she's smart she'll be able to control him. I knew this girl at university who had a rich sugar daddy. He gave her everything: money, clothes, holidays . . . And he never even touched her. She just had to do herself with sex toys while he watched, and that was it. Like she said, she'd have been doing that stuff anyway.'

'Still gross.'

'Says the born-again bisexual.'

'Is that what I am?'

'Isn't it? We've both had sex with men, after all.'

'But is that how you think of yourself? As bisexual?'

'I don't think of myself as anything, but technically, I guess, yeah.'

'So what are you saying? That you still want to have sex with guys?'

She shrugs. 'There are worse sensations.'

'Fuck you, Oxana. Seriously, fuck you.'

'So you don't want to have sex with a man again? Ever?'

'I don't want to have sex with anyone except you.'

'Interesting.'

I fall for it, of course, as she knows I will. 'Why can you never, ever, *ever* say anything nice?'

She flicks a glance at me. 'Because it's so much more fun bullying you, obviously. You know I asked Dasha to ask around about Lara?'

I don't answer. The only news I want to hear about Lara is that she's dead.

'I did, anyway. And apparently she's been released from Butyrka for lack of evidence. Her case isn't going to court any more.'

'Well, whoopee for Russia's incorruptible justice system. Are you going to get in touch with her?'

'No. Why would I do that?'

'You're always going on about her.'

'Only to make you jealous, dumbass. Lara was good at sex, but she was quite stupid. I remember when we were in Venice, having dinner at our hotel, and I ordered us the lobster risotto, which was like the *specialità della casa*, and the sommelier asked us what wine we'd like and Lara said she wanted Baileys Irish Cream. I mean I'm sorry, but that's just disgusting. We were kissing later on and I could taste it on her tongue.'

'Thanks for that little detail. I've been trying not to think of you and her in Venice.'

She shrugs. 'It happened. And I have to admit that I do like pineapple on pizza.'

'That really is disgusting.'

'I'll take you to Hank's, in Paris. It's super-delicious.'

'I'm not sure I'd want to try it, even in Paris.'

'Oh boo, you prude. How I ever got you into bed I don't know.'

'You didn't "get" me into bed.'

'Oh, you think not?'

'I jumped. I wasn't pushed.'

'Is that right?'

'It is right. And I'm definitely not eating pineapple pizza.'

'We'll see about that. But back to Zoya's place. Getting inside the apartment when the Pakhan's there would be hard; the door's reinforced and there's a high-definition security camera. There's no way he'd let Zoya buzz a stranger in. Much easier to shoot Dzabrati and the bodyguard inside the building but outside the apartment, in one of the public areas. Ideally when they're leaving, and walking from the apartment to the elevator.'

'How do you get into the building?'

'I've found out that there's a single man living on the second floor who teaches at one of the universities and is regularly visited by one of his female students. I know both their names, and I could pretend to be a friend of hers with an urgent message for him. That would get me inside. Then I could immobilise him, and take things from there. Not ideal, but possible.'

'The restaurant?'

'Again, possible. I could walk in, shoot the Pakhan in the face, do a couple of the bodyguards before they can react, and fuck off fast. But big, popular restaurants like Zarina are bad news. They're crowded, they're well lit, and there's CCTV. It would be messy, and there would be a lot of witnesses.'

'Witnesses would definitely be bad news.'

'Exactly. We've got to find a solution that doesn't involve killing the bodyguards or any of the other soldiers. Dasha will never be able to keep the gang's trust and loyalty if they know she's been responsible for the death of their colleagues. Basically, we've got to get the Pakhan alone, and eliminate him without anyone seeing.'

'He's alone in the *banya*, we know that. And defenceless.'

'And how do you suggest that I, or we, get into the bath-house? On the days he goes it's men only.'

'There must be a way.'

Oxana frowns. 'I spent hours in there on one of the women's days. I know the layout of the entire place. I checked out cupboards, ceiling cavities, ventilation ducts, everything like that, and there's literally nowhere to hide. The place is well over a hundred years old, built in Tsarist times, with mosaics and classical statues. And there are customers everywhere.'

'Naked guys with towels around their waists.'

'Well, women on the day I was there. But yeah.'

'So no guns.'

'It's next to impossible to conceal a gun in a bathhouse.'

'Tell me the routine again.'

'Why?'

'Oxana, please, just tell me.'

'OK. You go in through the street entrance, pay your money at the ticket-desk, and go into a big changing room with lockers, where you leave your clothes and collect your towel. Then you go through to the steam rooms. These have fire-boxes in them, like giant ovens with hot rocks inside, and wooden benches round the walls where you sit. There's a bucket, which you fill from a tap and pour into the fire-box through a hole. This produces the steam which raises the heat.'

'Like a sauna?'

'Same. Except everything's bigger. And it's more sociable than a European sauna, where everyone just sits in silence. Then there's a kind of cooling-off room with steel pillars and marble slabs where you can get a massage, and people smack each other with birch twigs, which is supposed to be good for the circulation.' Oxana folds her arms. 'Eve, you know all this, I've described it to you before.'

'I know you have. Tell me again. I'm just trying to figure something out.'

'OK, there's also a room with a small plunge pool.'

'Hot or cold?'

'Cold. You go there from the steam room.'

'How big is it?'

'It's just for one person. About a metre and a half deep.'

'What else does the place offer?'

'There's a tea room with a samovar. You can get cakes and blinis and stuff.'

'Good quality?'

'Pretty good.'

'What did you have?'

'A slice of Napoleon cake.'

'Just one slice?'

'OK, two.'

'So you wouldn't mind necessarily going back there? And taking me?'

'No. But since we're never going to get in there on a men's day, I don't see the point.'

'Bear with me, OK? I've got an idea.'

'I'm listening.'

So I tell her. Afterwards she sits there for a minute, unmoving. Then she walks slowly but agitatedly to the window, making fluttering gestures with her fingers.

'What do you think?'

She turns round. 'It could work. If Dasha can get us everything we need, it could definitely work.'

'But?'

'But it would take both of us. You'd have to be part of it. So . . .'

'So?'

'Are you ready to do it? Killing's a one-way door. There's no going back.'

'I'm ready.'

She stares at me for a heartbeat, and nods. 'OK.'

'Oxana?'

'Yes?'

'Try not to be such a bitch. We could be a good team.'

'Fine. Run that bath.'

With the plan finalised, and the arrangements made, Oxana and I suddenly have time on our hands. We go for long walks together, especially in Kupchino, the outlying district from which Dasha's gang gets its name. It's a tough place, a wilderness of deteriorating concrete housing blocks intersected by motorway viaducts and frozen canals. Cut off from the city by an industrial sprawl to the north, the windy streets resemble an abandoned moon colony, but with little sign of a police presence or CCTV cameras we feel safe here. This is Dasha's fiefdom, and when the monolithic grey outlines of the housing blocks soften in the rose-pink twilight at the end of the day, it's almost beautiful.

Much of our walking is done in silence. Sometimes we don't speak for an hour, just march side by side beneath cold skies criss-crossed with power and tram cables. We are learning each other. Sometimes I look at her and she's there with me, fully present; sometimes she's blank-eyed, in a dimension all her own. She's trying hard to be considerate, even though it doesn't come at all naturally to her. So she'll suddenly stop beside me on the pavement and gently wipe the snow from my face with her gloved hand, or ask me odd, sweet questions like whether I'm happy, or want a cup of tea. Seeing the determined, slightly perplexed look in her eyes at these moments I want to hug her, but I know that this would infringe her rules about attracting attention in public. So I tell her, truthfully, that I'm happy. I don't think about the killing that lies ahead. I think about now, and the two of us, and the tiny, elusive glimmer of her kindness.

It's Monday, nine days later, and Dasha has just learnt that the Pakhan has ordered his driver to take him from the apartment on Malaya Balkanskaya directly to the Elizarova *banya*. This works well for Oxana and me. We have everything we need in place, and it's already snowing heavily this afternoon, which will compromise the effectiveness of the CCTV cameras in the streets surrounding the bathhouse.

We leave the apartment at midday for Kupchino station, and take the Metro two stops northwards to Moskovskaya. Our vehicle is waiting for us outside Alfa Bank, as agreed. It's a Gazelle ambulance, about ten years old, with the interior fixtures stripped out but with emergency lights and siren still in place. According to Dasha, 'ambulance-taxis' like this one are regularly hired by wealthy business types who want to beat St Petersburg's traffic jams and get to meetings on time. With their sirens blaring and their lights blazing, they can thread their way through the worst gridlocks.

Pulling on latex gloves we take the keys from the top of the rear wheel, where the owner has left them, and open up the Gazelle. After checking the equipment, we change into official blue ambulance-crew uniforms, and pull on our wigs and cotton caps. Oxana's wig is a garish henna-red, mine peroxide blonde. Oxana drives. We've left ourselves plenty of time, so she takes the slow lane on the eastbound motorway, impassively negotiating the busy traffic. She radiates calm, her eyes betraying nothing except anticipation. As for me, I'm all over the place. One moment I'm intensely focused, with my surroundings vibrant and pin-sharp. The next everything is flat and two-dimensional, and I'm so distanced from events it's as if my life is being lived by someone else.

We're in position by quarter to two. Oxana parks in the narrow street that runs alongside the Elizarova *banya*, thirty metres from the entrance, and we put our feet up on the dashboard and wait for the Pakhan's arrival. My heart is slamming in my chest, and I feel weightless and nauseated. He arrives just two minutes before two o'clock, climbing from a black Mercedes SUV, and I switch on my phone to access the app controlling the microcamera that we planted in the bathhouse three days ago. The motion-activated camera is the size of my thumbnail, and it's held in place by a blob of chewing gum the size of a cherry stone.

79

To my horror I get a low-battery warning on the phone. Three per cent charge remaining. *Fuck*. I tell Oxana, my heart sinking. She doesn't waste time getting angry with me for forgetting to recharge it, but just nods, all focus. The seconds and minutes crawl past, agonisingly slowly. Two per cent battery charge left. The Pakhan will not visit the plunge pool, where the camera is hidden, until he has been through all the steam rooms. I touch the app icon, and a grainy image of the pool fills the phone screen. There's someone in the pool, a big guy, wallowing like a whale, and definitely not the Pakhan. He hauls himself out and vanishes. His place is taken by two older men who descend the ladder one by one, briefly immerse themselves, and leave.

There's now one per cent of the battery charge remaining, and the pool's empty. Another few minutes and the phone's going to die. I feel sick with dread. Fear of letting Oxana down has eclipsed all thought of our real purpose here. We stare at the tiny screen. Oxana's breathing is steady. Her wig, which smells of ancient sweat, tickles my cheek. A figure enters the microcamera's field at the same moment that the screen goes black.

'Go,' says Oxana, grabbing the first-aid pack and the medication bag. 'Go, go, go.'

I take a firm grip on the defibrillator unit. It's the mono-phasic type, at least twenty years old, and heavy. Oxana pushes open the side door of the Gazelle, we hit the pavement running, and seconds later burst through the entrance of the *banya*. There are two male reception staff sitting at a desk behind a low pile of folded towels. Seeing us they half-rise, and Oxana yells at them to stay where they are.

They look uncertain, but our uniforms represent official-dom, and they obey.

Oxana leads the way, marching briskly through the changing room, ignoring the half-naked figures who freeze with surprise at the sight of us, and into the wet-floored steam rooms. Here, again, everyone stares and no one moves. The choking heat makes my scalp run with sweat, and my glasses steam up so that I can't see where I'm going. Grabbing my arm, Oxana drags me into the cold plunge area, I wipe my glasses on my shirt, and there's the Pakhan, alone and naked, submerged up to his chest in the small marble pool. He has an impressive range of faded tattoos, including a knife through his neck, eight-pointed stars on his collarbones, and epaulettes on his shoulders.

'Are you all right?' I ask him breathlessly. 'We had a 112 call.'

He gapes at me, understanding neither the situation nor, probably, my shaky Russian. Oxana, meanwhile, drops everything she's carrying, and attends to the defibrillator.

'I'm fine,' the Pakhan says, smiling. 'There's been some mistake.'

'Our apologies,' Oxana murmurs, and touches the defibrillator paddles to the surface of the water. The Pakhan shudders, his eyes widen, and he slips sideways onto his back, his legs trailing underwater. His face turns the colour of putty, and his lips bluish-grey. His fingers twitch and grasp feebly at the water. His hands, I notice, are quite small for a man who has killed several people with an axe.

'Bit more?' I suggest.

'Stand back,' Oxana says, and gives him another jolt of electricity.

Still Dzabrati doesn't die. Instead he lies there open-mouthed, pillowed by water, staring at me sadly as if disappointed by my choice of wig. So I kneel, take Oxana's wrist with one hand to steady myself, and hold his head under-water with the other until the bubbles stop coming. It's nothing much. I don't even have to push very hard.

I'm still kneeling there when, with a wet slap of plastic sandals, the two reception staff arrive. 'I think he's had a heart attack,' Oxana explains. 'We're trying to get him out. Can you help?'

One of the men descends the ladder into the water, and between them they manhandle the Pakhan's naked body onto the tiled floor. As they do so Oxana discreetly reaches up and removes the micro camera from the top of the door frame. Kneeling beside the wet body of the Pakhan, I go through the motions of attempting cardiopulmonary resuscitation. To no one's surprise, it doesn't work.

An hour later, Oxana and I are walking away from the ambulance, which we've left outside Alfa Bank in Moskovskaya, where we found it. We're back in our own clothes. The ambulance service uniforms, the wigs and the medical equipment have been tossed into the back of one of the city's garbage trucks, and are now on their way to a landfill site.

'I'm really sorry about the phone . . .' I begin, but Oxana is in an affectionate, almost light-headed mood. I'm wearing my black and yellow sweater under my leather jacket and she calls me *pchelka*, her bee. 'You were so good,' she says, slipping her arm through mine and dancing us down Moskovsky Avenue towards the Metro. 'You really kept your shit together. I'm super-proud of you.'

Deciding that she's hungry, Oxana steers us into a half-empty McDonald's, where we order Happy Meals. 'People think that there's this hard border between life and death,' she says, cramming fries into her mouth. 'But it's not like that at all. There's this whole area in between. It's fascinating.'

I unwrap my burger. Our faces are inches apart. 'Did Dasha say when she could get us the papers and the money?'

'Yes. This week.'

'So do we have a plan?'

'Yes, we absolutely do.'

'What is it?'

'You have to trust me, *pchelka*.'

'No, you have to trust me, remember?'

'Oh yes, so I do. OK, well . . . Can we talk about it this evening?'

'Why not now?'

I feel a hand slip under my sweater, and fingers tweaking my waist.

'That's not an answer. And stop pinching my fat.'

'I love your fat.'

'What about the rest of me?'

'Hmm . . .' She half-turns. 'Oh my goodness, look at that face. I'm teasing you.'

'Funny girl. So what shall we do?'

Her hand continues its exploration. I feel the tip of a finger probing my belly button. 'Let's go back to the apartment.'

'Why?'

'You know why.'

I take a bite of my burger. The greasy smell hangs in the air between us. 'It's not really about me, though, is it? It's what we did in the *banya* that's making you want sex.'

'Honestly? It's both.' She wipes her chin with a paper napkin.

'So what is it that excites you about killing that nasty old fucker? I mean, it was pretty disgusting.'

'This hamburger's pretty disgusting, *pupsik*, but sometimes that's exactly what you want. You can't live on beluga caviar.'

'Go on.'

'Killing people like the Pakhan makes me feel powerful. Konstantin always used to say: "You're an instrument of destiny." And I loved that. I love that I've changed history, and that if it wasn't for me the world would be a different place. Because in the end, that's what we all dream of doing, isn't it? Making a difference?'

Half-a-dozen blue-uniformed *Politsiya* officers swagger in, give a cursory glance around the restaurant, and start eyeing up the women at the serving counter. 'Don't look at them,' murmurs Oxana, surreptitiously sliding her hand from under my sweater, and I transfer my gaze to a copy of *Izvestia* that someone's left on the table. The lead story is about the upcoming New Year summit talks in Moscow between the Russian and US presidents.

One of the cops saunters over. 'Afternoon off work?' He's a mean-looking type with a bad shaving rash.

'Tourists,' says Oxana in English. '*Ne govorim po Russki*.' Her accent is comically awful.

'*Ty amerikanets?*'

'British.'

'*Pasport?*'

'At the Hotel. Four Seasons. *Sozhaleyu*. Sorry.'

He nods and joins the others.

'Motherfucker,' Oxana whispers. 'We shouldn't have come in here. I think they bought the tourist story, but that could have ended badly. We've got to be more careful.'

The *Politsiya* officers mill around for a few minutes, attempt desultory banter with the female staff, pull out their phones and take selfies, and leave.

'What were they doing in here?' Oxana mutters. 'What the fuck were they doing, taking those photos? Did you notice that they didn't get any food? Or even a drink?'

'They were just getting in out of the cold for a minute, and checking out the girls.'

'Maybe. I hope so.'

'You know what I'd really like to do?' I tell her. 'I'd like to go into the city centre. St Petersburg has got to be one of the most beautiful cities in the world, and I've dreamed of visiting it for ages, especially in winter. The palaces, the art galleries . . . Just to walk down the streets, and see the frozen Neva river. It must be so magical.'

'I know. I'd love to see it all too. And one day we will. But right now the centre's too dangerous. There's mass-surveillance tech everywhere – CCTV, facial recognition scanners, all that stuff – and we have to assume the Twelve are monitoring it and have flags out for us. And that goes for every big city in the world. For now, we've got to stick to outlying areas.'

'Promise me we'll come back one day, and explore it together. Promise me that.'

'OK.'

'Say it. I promise . . .'

'I promise that we'll come back to St Petersburg, and walk together by the Neva—'

'In winter, in the snow.'

'Yes, in winter. In the snow.'

'You really and truly promise?'

'I really and truly promise. But you have to promise me something too.'

'What?'

'You have to trust me. I mean really trust me, despite the . . .'

'Psychopath thing?'

'Yes, despite that. Even if things get really bad.'

'Villa . . . Oxana, you're frightening me. What do you mean?'

'I mean trust me. That's all.'

'I'm scared now.'

'Don't be. Let's do what we should have done an hour ago, and go back to the apartment and have sex.'

'My silver-tongued girlfriend.'

'What's that about my tongue?'

'It's an English expression. It means you have a way with words. You know how to talk a woman into bed.'

'That's true.'

'So what would you have done if I'd said no. If we'd run away together and all that and then I'd refused to do it.'

'Do it?'

'Sleep with you. Have sex. Be your girlfriend.'

'I always knew you'd do all of those things.'

'How did you know? I mean, I was married, I had a husband, I'd never so much as looked at a woman . . .'

'You looked at me. And I looked back.'

'And what did you see?'

'You, *pchelka*.'

# 6

At 5 p.m. Asmat Dzabrati's family are contacted by officials of Pokrovskaya Hospital with a request to collect his body. There is, apparently, no suggestion that the Pakhan died of anything other than natural causes, although there is some confusion about the fact that two ambulance teams appear to have attended the bathhouse where he suffered a fatal heart attack. This is Russia, however, and such misunderstandings occur. Pokrovskaya is a busy public hospital, and the duty physician who certified Dzabrati dead on arrival from the Elizarova *banya*, and issued the requisite certificates, saw no reason to authorise a post-mortem examination. Apart from anything else, it appears that the mortuary is full. All of this is relayed to us by Dasha, following her long and difficult phone conversation with Dzabrati's tearful ex-wife Yelena. Dasha then convenes an emergency meeting of the three other Kupchino Bratva brigadiers, who arrive within the hour.

Kris, Oxana and I have dinner in the kitchen. After winding herself around me like a cat all afternoon, and practically dragging me into bed, Oxana is now in a simmering fury. When we sit down to eat, she sips Dasha's vintage Riesling, announces that it tastes like petrol, and helps herself to champagne from the fridge. I know better than to ask why she's so angry, but I'm certain that it's because she hasn't been invited to attend Dasha's gangster conclave. Though why she thinks she should be invited, I have no idea. So as Kris and I dart anxious glances at each other, Oxana spoons down her borscht with sour cherries, scours out the bowl with a hunk of bread, flips her spoon into the sink, and walks out without a word.

'Sorry,' I say. 'Again.'

Kris nods. 'There are things Dasha doesn't tell me, but I'm not stupid. I know that you and Oxana were involved in what happened today. I'm not going to ask you about it, but I just want you to know that I know.'

'OK. Thank you.'

'Are you all right? Oxana's obviously dealing with it in her own way, but—'

'I think I'm OK. I'm not sure.'

'Was it awful?'

'Not really. If I'm honest.'

Kris peels a banana. 'She loves you. You know that, don't you?'

'I wonder. There are times when I think that she just conceivably might do. Then there are others when it's hard to believe that she even likes me.'

'Eve, you prove to Oxana that she exists. You're the only reality that she has outside herself. It's that basic.'

'You think her insecurity's that deep?'

'I do, yeah. You're going soon, aren't you?'

'I guess.'

'I know. Dasha's got your passports and money in our room. She's had them for two days. I'll miss you.'

'I'll miss you too, Kris. How do you feel about Dasha becoming the Pakhan?'

Kris shrugs her narrow shoulders. 'It's what she wants, although I've never understood why. I mean, fuck. Those *bratva* guys. They're jackals. You take your eyes off them for a second, and they rip you apart.' She looks away. 'I have a lot to be grateful for, Eve, truly. And unlike Zoya, I don't have to sleep with some horrible old guy to support myself. But I worry. I worry all the time.'

'About?'

'About this life. About the *vorovskoy mir*. Gang leaders don't grow old.' She winds the banana skin around her finger. 'I love Dasha and I don't want to see her die.'

'I'd say she can look after herself pretty well, having seen her in action.'

'At the factory, you mean?'

'Sorry, I didn't mean to bring it up. And we did make a mess. I still feel bad about that.'

'Don't. The whole place burnt down earlier this week. There was literally nothing left, so the insurance claim will be massive. But bring your glass. There's something I want to show you.'

She takes me into the bedroom she shares with Dasha. I've never been in here before and I look around with amazement. The bed is a four-poster with purple damask curtains, the walls are decorated with framed posters of Amazonian women riding dinosaurs and giant dragonflies, the shelves hold velveteen unicorns, Beanie Babies and statuettes of Marvel Comic heroines.

'This look is more you than Dasha, isn't it?'

'She said I could have it how I wanted. What do you think?'

'Cool. I'm guessing your side of the bed is the one without the gun.'

Kris shoves the butt of the Serdyukov automatic under the pillow. 'You guess right. I hate that it's there, but she insists. Apart from that, I love it in here. It's where I come when everything gets too much.' She gestures for me to make myself comfortable on the bed, then turns down the light, takes a DVD from a shelf, and slips it into the player. It's a cartoon, very old-fashioned, about a hedgehog going to meet his friend, a bear cub, so that they can count the stars in the sky. Thinking that he has seen a beautiful white horse, the hedgehog tries to follow it and gets lost in the night.

The film is short, lasting perhaps ten minutes, and when it ends Kris's eyes are shining with tears. 'What did you think?' she asks me.

'It's sweet.'

'I just love it. I feel like that all the time. Like I'm lost in the fog, and all I can see are the outlines of monsters. But it ends happily. The hedgehog is saved, and he finds his friend, and they count the stars together, like they always do. And that's all I want to do, really. Count the stars with Dasha.'

I don't know what to say, so I reach for her hand. 'You will,' I tell her.

In the bedroom Oxana is asleep in one of my T-shirts. The curtains are undrawn, and on the boulevard outside the fresh snow glitters beneath the street lights. Oxana's face is turned towards the window, and I watch the flutter of her lashes as she dreams. What stories is her mind creating? Am I there with her?

I pull the covers over her. Her eyes don't open but her hand snakes out and her fingers lock around my wrist, strong as steel. 'G'night, bitch,' she murmurs, and starts to snore.

The next morning Dasha joins us for breakfast. 'It's been great having you,' she tells us. 'And thank you for your help with my predecessor. But you need to leave St Petersburg today. I'm the acting Pakhan of the Kupchino Bratva now, so . . .'

Dasha doesn't need to finish. We all know what she means. She's discharged her duty to us, just as we have to her. Now it is time to go, before our presence makes life complicated for her. 'Your passports,' she says, handing Oxana an envelope.

'Thank you. I won't forget what you've done for us.'

Dasha gives me one of her sharp little smiles. 'Sorry about hanging you up by the wrists. Must have been uncomfortable.'

'I did punch you on the nose.'

'You did, didn't you.'

Back in our room, Oxana and I pack our rucksacks and inspect the passports. These appear to be new, and issued in the names of Maria Bogomolova and Galina Tagaeva. I'm Galina.

It takes us very little time to get ready to go. We've decided to take the train to Sochi, a modern city on the Black Sea, find a cheap guest house, and review our options. I'm sad to be saying goodbye to Kris. She and I have become good friends in the time we've been staying here, and I decide to give her the blue velvet coat from the Mikhailovsky Theatre. Kris is touchingly excited – I know that she wishes she'd seen it first at the Kometa vintage store – and she puts it on at once, posing self-consciously. Dasha accompanies us to the entrance hall of the building. I shake her hand, unsure of the protocol, while she and Oxana exchange a fleeting hug. Kris, looking like a minor character from *Anna Karenina* in the velvet coat, steps out of the front door. She's walking with us to the Metro station. There's been no snowfall this morning, and Kris stands there for a moment, a slight, wistful figure. The wind blows an escaping tendril of hair across her face, and she's lifting her free hand to brush it away when there's a smacking sound, not loud, and she lifts from the pavement and flies back through the open door like a blown leaf, landing on her side between Dasha and me.

'Get inside,' Oxana says, wrenching me away from the entrance. 'Dasha, *move.*' But Dasha's on her knees, gazing at Kris's surprised eyes and twitching body. As I back away towards the stairs, I see the fist-sized hole and the mess of blood, bone and velvet below her left shoulder.

'Dasha,' I say, my voice shaking.

Still she doesn't move. Then she slips an arm below her dying lover's knees and another below her shoulders, and lifts her like a sleeping child from the widening pool of blood.

'Get upstairs,' Oxana orders. Her Sig Sauer's in her hand, and her eyes are as flat as a snake's.

When they've gone, Oxana and I grab our rucksacks and race through unlit corridors to the rear of the building.

Outside, visible through heavy glass-panelled doors, is a snow-covered car park and garbage collection area. Oxana gives it a single wary glance and pulls me back the way we came.

'They'll have it covered,' she says. 'We've got to go back up to the apartment. We need the service staircase.'

'Who are "they"?' I ask Oxana, and she just looks at me. We both know who they are.

The Twelve have found us.

By the time we get upstairs Kris is dead. Dasha carried her body to their bedroom, and when she emerges, her face like stone, she's all business. She hits the phone, issuing orders and summoning her soldiers from their various apartments in the building. Oxana, meanwhile, crouches at one of the front-facing windows, scanning the street with a pair of binoculars. I busy myself checking and re-checking my Glock, and keeping out of the others' way. I'm light-headed with shock. I keep thinking about Kris's coat. The coat that I've worn at least every other day for the last fortnight. The coat that I gave her.

'We have three men in a black Mercedes,' Oxana says after a couple of minutes. 'I'm pretty sure they're . . . Yes, they're all armed. Getting out of the car. Approaching the building now.'

As she finishes speaking, there's an urgent triple buzz at the front door of the apartment. It's three of the *boyeviks*, carrying automatic weapons and spare magazines. Dasha hurries them in, a heavy Makarov pistol in her hand, and issues a terse series of orders. Two of the soldiers return through the front door to take up position on the stairs and landing outside, the third starts upending tables and heavy furniture in the apartment's entrance hall. Oxana, meanwhile, runs around switching off lights and pulling curtains closed. In a firefight darkness favours those who know the terrain.

'It's me they want,' I tell Dasha, suddenly sure of my words. 'They shot Kris because she was wearing my coat. Send me out to them. Please, don't risk anyone else's life.'

Dasha frowns distractedly. 'Go to my bedroom,' she says. 'Shut yourself in.'

'Do it, Eve,' Oxana confirms, and I obey. I feel as if I'm sleepwalking, as if I'm no longer in charge of the business of putting one leg in front of the other.

Kris, her eyes still open, has been laid out on her back on the double bed. The ghastly exit wound can't be seen. The only visible sign of the shot that killed her is a neat hole in the blue velvet coat, over her heart.

Seeing her there, surrounded by her fairy posters and unicorn statuettes, I begin to weep. I feel so lost, so useless, so guilty. I know that Oxana, Dasha and the bodyguards know what they're doing, and that I'd only be in the way, but this powerlessness is horrible, particularly since I'm responsible for Kris's death. And then there's Dasha. I don't warm to her, but Oxana and I have brought nothing into her life except mayhem, and the vengeance of the Twelve. And now Dasha is putting her life on the line to defend us.

From the street, far below, I hear a faint splintering, as the attackers kick in the front door of the building. It's followed by a sporadic popping sound, at first distant, but soon rising in volume as the *boyeviks* engage the attackers. I should feel fear, but I don't. Sitting on the bed, loaded weapon in hand, I feel nothing except a flat sadness. From the other end of the apartment there's a shattering crash as the front door gives way, followed by confused shouting and staccato bursts of gunfire. Someone is screaming, and although I know that it's not Oxana's voice I'm weak with terror at the thought of losing her. The screaming dies to an intermittent groaning.

I have to help. Or at least try to.

Touching my pocket to check for spare Glock magazines, I make for the door, and turn the key with trembling fingers. Outside a passage leads to the darkened reception room where we gathered before dinner with the late Pakhan.

As I step into the passage, the tears drying on my cheeks, a ringing silence prevails. There's the crack of a handgun from the entrance hall, shockingly amplified in the enclosed space, and silence again. I creep through the reception room, fearfully hugging the wall, and edge towards the open door and the entrance hall beyond. This is also dark, but I can make out the main features. Just metres in front of me, a marble-topped table has been pushed on its side, spilling a pair of heavy onyx lamps onto the floor, and behind the tabletop, in profile, crouch two men dressed in street clothes and armed with sub-machine guns. Beyond this pair, his body slumped over the vertical tabletop as if arrested in the course of a dive, is a third man. I can't see who is facing them at the other end of the hall but I pray that one of them is Oxana.

Buried in darkness, breathing air sharp with gun smoke, I attempt to take stock. I don't recognise the man nearest me; he could be one of Dasha's soldiers. Then I see the pale chevrons of impacted snow on the treads of his combat boots. He's just come in from the street. He's an attacker and I decide to kill him, or try to. '. . . *if we're going to survive, you're going to have to be a bit more like me.*'

Very slowly, I raise the Glock, lining up foresight, backsight and the man's ear.

*And the second guy?* It's as if she's whispering in my ear.

I'll deal with him next, I promise her, and squeeze the Glock's trigger.

I don't kill him. The 9mm round smashes a hank of hair and bone from the back of his head, and as he whips round to face me, sub-machine gun levelled, Oxana rises into view on the far side of the room and fires two shots in fast succession. Both rounds punch through the man's throat and he sinks to the floor, choking.

The second man returns fire but Oxana has vanished. He turns to me, and I squeeze off a round that tears through his cheek and rips one ear from his face. There's a flare of orange at his gun barrel, and a fiery whiplash streaks across my back. I'm dimly aware of the crack of a third weapon – Dasha's Makarov – and watch detachedly as his knees fold and a slew of brain matter pours from the side of his head.

Dasha and Oxana rise to their feet, and Oxana races across to where I'm lying. 'You dumbass!' she screams. 'You fucking idiot.'

'My back. I've been hit.'

'Sit up. Let me look.' She switches on the reception room lights, pulls off my leather jacket, and wrenches my blood-sodden sweater over my head. Sprawled in front of me in the unlit hall, just a few metres away, the three attackers lie in twisted, grotesque repose. The second attacker is still alive, and his eyes follow Dasha as she walks over to him, slaps a fresh magazine into her pistol, and fires a single shot through the base of his nose. Then she heads for the front door. 'I'm going to check the stairs. See if any of my people are still alive.'

'OK,' Oxana says.

I'm so sick with guilt I can't even look at Dasha, let alone respond. I think of Kris, lying lifeless in their bedroom.

Oxana walks away, returning with a military-issue first-aid box and a wet bath towel. It's very cold, and as she cleans up my back I feel savage waves of pain. 'You were lucky,' she murmurs. 'A centimetre deeper and you'd have been paralysed. Dasha saved your life. What the fuck were you thinking? We told you to—'

'I know you did. I wanted to help.'

'And I guess you did help. But Jesus, Eve.'

'I know. Everything's fucked.'

'Just don't move.' She presses the towel hard against my back. 'I thought I'd lost you, you stupid bitch.'

'I'm sorry,' I repeat.

'You will be, because I'm going to stitch you.' She kneels beside me and sets to work with a suturing needle. It hurts a lot, but I'm glad of the pain. It means I don't have to think.

'Have you done this before?' I murmur.

'No, but we did sewing at school. I made a crocodile. It had teeth and everything.'

Dasha walks back into the flat, her face wiped of all expression. She's accompanied by two men and a woman, and she's no longer holding the Makarov. That's now in the right hand of a strongly built young woman with cropped blonde hair, broad features, and eyes the colour of slate.

I recognise her instantly from a CCTV clip that we had on file in Goodge Street. Lara Farmanyants, Oxana's former lover and companion in murder, recently released from Butyrka jail. Beside Lara, cradling a sub-machine gun, is the man I know as Anton, formerly a squadron commander in the Special Air Service and now the head of the Twelve's 'housekeeping' or assassination department. The second man is Richard Edwards, my former boss at MI6, and a long-term Twelve asset.

Pain folds into paralysing despair. It's over.

When they've disarmed us, the newcomers look around them, registering the upturned furniture, the bodies, the spattered walls, and the congealing pools of blood. All three appear entirely at home among the carnage.

'So,' Oxana says, continuing to stitch my back. 'You.'

'Me,' Lara replies.

In the clip, sent to us by the Italian police, she and Oxana were strolling down the Calle Vallaresso in Venice, window-shopping. With her straw cowboy hat tilted just so, Lara looked like a catwalk model. In the flesh, with a state-of-the-art sniper rifle slung across her chest and Dasha's Makarov in her hand, she looks a lot more dangerous.

'Is she the one who killed Kristina?' Dasha asks, her voice so low I can hardly hear her.

'*Are they* the one,' Lara corrects her. 'My pronouns are "they" and "them" now. But yeah, that was me. Sorry.'

Dasha frowns. I know that she wants to scream, to hurl herself at Lara and inflict agonising violence on her. But she is a Pakhan, and does none of these things. 'Just know this,' she says to Lara. 'I will kill you. That's a promise.'

'You've already killed three of our soldiers,' Richard says. 'For a local *bratva*, that's impressive.'

Dasha turns to Oxana, her green eyes steady. 'These are your people?'

'Not any more.' I feel her pull the final stitch tight.

'You've heard of *Dvenadsat*?' says Richard. 'The Twelve?'

'I've heard of them,' says Dasha. 'So?'

'So you've been extending your hospitality to two people with whom we have issues, Miss Kvariani. Mrs Polastri here, my none-too-bright former employee. And her somewhat unstable girlfriend.' He inclines his head in our direction.

'And for this you murder an innocent young woman, storm my building with assault weapons, seriously injure two of the men who are trying to defend me, and kill a third? Fuck you and fuck your Twelve.'

'Our condolences for the loss of the girl. That was unintentional.' He looks at Lara. 'She mistook her for Eve.'

'They mistook her,' says Lara.

'Your *condolences*?' My voice shakes. 'You have a daughter her age, Richard. How would you feel if someone shot Chloe, and then turned to you and said it was "unintentional"? You fucking monster.'

Richard ignores me and continues to address Dasha. 'All that we want from you is Villanelle.'

'Who's Villanelle?' Dasha asks.

'I used to be,' says Oxana. 'Long story.'

'She's ours,' says Richard. 'Bought and paid for.'

'Wrong, asshole,' Oxana says. 'Those days are over.'

Richard flicks her a brief smile and switches his gaze to me. He's wearing a velvet-collared overcoat and beneath it an old school tie, black with a pale-blue stripe.

'So, did Kim Philby go to Eton too?' I ask him.

'No. Westminster. Bit of an oik, our Kim. And a traitor of course, which I'm not.'

'And how are you not a traitor, Richard, may I ask?'

'If I could show you the big picture, Eve, you'd understand. But right now none of us has the time for that.' He moves away from me and cursorily examines the three dead men on the floor. 'You'll be glad to know that your attempt to fake your own death delayed us for a whole twenty-four hours. A convincing piece of work. We allowed your husband a glimpse of the photograph, and he was quite upset. This time, though, it's going to be for real. Anton, would you kindly do the honours?'

Anton takes Oxana's Sig from his pocket, and weighs it in his hands. 'No. I've got a better idea.' Popping out the Sig's magazine, he removes all the rounds except one, and then hands the gun to Oxana.

'Villanelle, shoot Eve in the head. Quickly please.'

My mind empties. At least it'll be her.

'Get on with it,' Anton says.

Oxana doesn't move. She's calm, her breathing steady. She stares at the Sig, frowning.

'Am I going to have to do it myself?' Anton says. 'Because I'd be very happy to. I just thought it might be more intimate this way.' He regards us with fastidious distaste. 'I know how . . . fond you two are of each other.'

102

'If anyone harms Eve, I'll shoot myself,' Oxana answers, raising the Sig and pressing the barrel to her temple. 'I'm serious. I'll blow my brains across the room.'

Richard gives her the thinnest of smiles. 'Villanelle, we have a job for you. The one that all the others have been leading up to.'

'And if I say no?'

'You won't say no. This will be the greatest challenge of your career. And afterwards, you'll be free to go, with more money than you'll ever be able to spend.'

'Of course. You'd really let me go.'

'We really would. The world would be a different place.'

'And Eve?'

'Right now, her knowledge threatens us all. Kill her and move on.'

'No. Eve comes with me.'

Richard regards her patiently. 'Villanelle, there are other women. This one's really very ordinary. She'll hold you back.'

Her eyes a frozen grey, Oxana returns the barrel of the Sig to her temple. 'Eve lives. Agree, or I fire.'

Anton regards her expressionlessly for a moment. 'If Eve lives, you accept the contract.'

'Who's the target?'

'You'll learn in due course. But I guarantee that you'll be impressed.'

'And if I'm not?'

'If you decline the contract, then you and your . . . *girl-friend*' – he says the word as if it nauseates him – 'will be loose ends that we have to tie up. And we will. No faked deaths, no last-minute escapes. Just two anonymous bodies in a landfill.' Swinging the barrel of his weapon towards me, as if to warn Oxana not to try anything, he takes back the Sig. 'But don't let's spoil the moment. You won't decline this one. And the really heart-warming news is that you'll be working with Lara again. She can't wait.'

'They can't wait,' says Lara.

# 7

We spend the rest of the day in the black Mercedes, travelling to Moscow. Anton drives, Richard is in the passenger seat, and Lara, Oxana and I are in the back. It's a perverse situation. My back hurts like hell, the slightest bump or vibration tearing at the stitches. Oxana gazes wordlessly out of the side window, Lara looks bored, and I sit between them, watching the flat, snow-blown landscape race past. Meanwhile, Oxana's Sig and my Glock are in Anton's pockets.

'. . . *shoot Eve in the head.*'

At intervals I find myself weeping, or shaking uncontrollably. When this happens Oxana looks at me with frowning concern. She doesn't know what to say or do. At random moments she takes my hand, wipes my eyes with a tissue, or puts an arm around me and presses my head awkwardly to her shoulder. Lara pointedly ignores all of this.

'*Kill her and move on.*'

I don't respond to Oxana. I can't. I'm locked in to the events of the morning. Kris's sudden weightlessness as she is borne backwards by the high-velocity sniper round, and the softness with which she falls to the marble floor. The sound of bullets smacking into clothing and flesh. The tiny blur of orange announcing the shot that furrows through my back, and the way that the sound seems to follow the pain. The sight of Dasha's men as we leave. One sprawled across the stairs, glued in place by his own congealed blood. Two others sitting on the half-landing, wounded but alive, and one of them, the one that Oxana struck on the head with her Sig Sauer, raising a rueful hand in farewell as we pass.

'. . . *shoot Eve in the head.*'

We pass exits for Gatchina, Tosno, Kirishi.

'*Quickly please.*'

Velikiy Novgorod, Borovichi.

'*Kill her and move on.*'

Oxana takes my head in her hands, and gently turns it until we are face to face. 'Listen to me,' she says, very quietly, so that only I can hear. 'I'm going to tell you a story. A story about my mother. Her name was Nadezhda, and she grew up on a farm, a few miles from the town of Novozybkov, although her family was originally from Chuvashia. She was very pretty, in the Chuvash way, with a high forehead and long dark hair. Something about her eyes, perhaps the arch of her brows, gave her a surprised expression. When she was fifteen there was the reactor meltdown at Chernobyl, a hundred and fifty kilometres away. The wind carried the radiation north-east to the Novozybkov district, and everyone from my mother's village was evacuated. Soon afterwards the area became a Closed Zone.

'I'm not sure how my mother ended up in Perm. Perhaps she was sent to relatives. She married my father when she was twenty-two, and I was born a year later. I was a very clever child, and I'm not sure how, but I always knew that Mama was sick, and would die before long. I hated her for that, for forcing this sadness on me, and sometimes at night I dreamed that the waiting was over and she was already dead. She looked so helpless, so vulnerable, and that made me angry too, because I knew that was not how things were supposed to be. She was supposed to look after me. She was supposed to teach me all the things I needed to know.

'There would often be whole days when she stayed in bed, and my father had to stay at home and make my meals. He was a military instructor, and he had no idea what to do with a little girl, so he taught me the things that he taught his men: how to fight and survive. My best memory with him is of going into the woods in the winter and trapping a rabbit. I must have been about six. He made me kill and skin the rabbit myself, and we cooked it on a fire in the snow. I was very proud of that.

'It wasn't long afterwards that my mother said she was feeling better, and took me on a day trip to the Kungur ice caves. It was a special treat, partly because of the outing itself, but mostly because I was getting my mother to myself for a whole day. I even got a new coat to wear. It was pink quilted nylon, with a hood, and a zip down the front.

'We caught a bus from the Central station in Perm. The journey took about two hours, and we had lunch at a café in Kungur. Hamburger and chips, with Coca-Cola to drink, a big treat. I didn't know what to expect from the caves. I didn't know what a cave was, and ice didn't sound very interesting because we lived with it for half the year. So I wasn't prepared when we actually went down inside the earth. There was a paved stone track, and it was like going into some secret fairy-tale kingdom. There were ice crystals hanging from the ceiling like spears, shining ice pillars and waterfalls, and rock pools as clear as glass. Everything was lit up with coloured lights. 'Is it magic?' I asked my mother, and she told me that it was. Later, when we were on the bus going home, I asked if the magic would make her better, and she said that maybe, just maybe, it would.

'She died a few weeks later, and for years I wasn't quite sure if I'd imagined or dreamed the whole thing. It was all so unlike anything else in my life. All I knew was that magic might work for some people – film stars, models, people like that – but it didn't work for ordinary people like my family. I didn't cry when my mother died. I couldn't.'

Oxana falls silent for a heartbeat or two. 'I never told anyone else that story.'

'Is it true?'

'Yes. At least I think it is. It was all so long ago. Now lean your head on my shoulder and sleep. It's still three hours until Moscow.'

'Yesterday,' I whisper. 'You were ready to die for me?'

'Go to sleep, *pupsik*.'

When I wake it's dark and we are crawling through an industrial suburb in heavy traffic. The motorway is awash with churned-up slush. Anton follows an exit sign reading Ramenki.

'Feeling better?' Oxana asks me.

'I'm not sure. Maybe.'

'Good. We need to eat.' She kicks the back of the driver's seat. 'Hey assholes, we're hungry. What are the plans for dinner?'

Richard and Anton look at each other.

'Anton, you toad-faced dildo, I'm talking to you. Which restaurant are you taking us to, because it fucking well better be good.'

'Is she always like this?' Richard asks Anton.

'She's always been a degenerate, yes. There was a time she used to behave more respectfully.'

'Suck my dick, bitch. Those days are over. Tell me where we're going.'

'Somewhere we can have a civilised, face-to-face conversation,' Richard says. 'We're going to have to work together here. We can't have the project compromised by personality issues. It's too important.'

We sit in silence as we wind through the suburbs. It's snowing again, and I listen to the soft thump of the windscreen wipers and the hiss of the slush beneath our wheels. The city's traffic is as chaotic as ever, and as we pass Moscow State University and cross the river, we're forced to slow to a crawl. The last few hundred metres take almost half an hour, but finally we pull up in front of a massive Stalinist block. Its grey frontage, pierced with archways, extends the length of the entire street.

We climb out and stretch cramped limbs. The building's vast impersonality fills me with dread. Its towers are so tall that they vanish into the night sky. I'm standing next to Oxana, my back throbbing painfully, when there's a whooshing crunch in front of me, and glittering slivers spatter my face. Grabbing my arm, Oxana drags me beneath one of the archways.

'What—'

'Falling icicle,' she says, and when I've wiped my glasses I see the shattered lumps in the snow, some the size of a baby's head.

'Fucking hell.'

'Yes. You have to watch out for those.'

Lara saunters over from the Mercedes, grinning. 'Another near miss?'

I don't answer. I can't. The idea of a spear of ice plummeting from the sky seems, at this moment, wholly unsurprising.

Anton jumps out of the driver's seat, regards Oxana and me irritably, and locks the Mercedes.

'Take your things and follow Lara,' he orders us. 'And no bullshit. Because I know for a fact that she'd love an excuse to shoot you.'

'They'd love an excuse.'

We follow Lara into a huge, dimly lit atrium from which passageways lead in multiple directions. There are marble pillars and classical details of the sort that you might find in an international railway station, but the overall effect is cheerless. A few people come and go, muffled against the winter weather, and no one seems perturbed by the fact that Lara is carrying a sniper's rifle and an automatic pistol. There's a shining trail of boot-prints to the nearest lift, but Lara avoids this and leads us to a small alcove, and inputs a code into a wall panel. A door slides back, revealing a glass and steel lift, which whisks us with sickening speed to the twelfth floor.

We emerge into a softly illuminated space, neither hot nor cold, dominated by armoured-glass windows and a huge Salvador Dalí painting of a tiger. There are doors to left and right, and a faintly ominous humming that might be the building's climate control system or distant machinery. Beyond the windows, far below, the dark form of the Moscow river winds between snowy parks and windblown embankments.

Lara touches a button beside the right-hand door and we are admitted by a young man in paramilitary uniform, who leads us along a corridor hung with abstract paintings in hues of ivory, scarlet and vermilion, their slashing brushstrokes so exactly like knife wounds that the stitches in my back start to ache. Several other men and women in business suits pass us in the corridor, before Lara lets Oxana into one of the rooms and pointedly leads me to another. It's painted dove grey, and undecorated except for a bronze statuette of a panther, which stands on a walnut side table.

'I'm afraid there's no complimentary dressing gown or slippers,' Lara tells me sourly. 'We weren't expecting you to still be alive. I will collect you for dinner in one hour.'

I ease myself into a sitting position on the bed. My back is screaming now. 'Can you get me a doctor?' I ask them.

'You have pain?'

'Yes.'

'Show me.'

In answer I ease my sweater over my head, pull up my T-shirt and turn my back to them.

'OK, looks sore.' They pause. 'Why does she like you so much?'

'Oxana? I really don't know.'

'All the time, even in bed, she was like Eve, Eve, Eve. So annoying. I've tried to kill you *twice* now.'

111

'I noticed.'

'*Die Another Day*. You saw that film?'

'No.'

'Rosamund Pike, super-cute. Pierce Brosnan, not so cute. You think I could be in a Bond film?'

'Definitely. There's always some crazy Russian with a butch haircut and a big-ass gun.'

Lara looks at me uncertainly. 'OK. I'll find someone.'

The doctor arrives just ten minutes later. A businesslike young woman in the uniform of a Russian navy medic, with a case full of gear. She prods the stitches, feels my lymph nodes, and gives me a box of antibiotic tablets and another of painkillers. She doesn't ask me how I came by an obvious gunshot wound, but she's interested in the stitches. 'Haven't seen that before. Blanket-stitch suturing. Nice neat work, though.'

'My girlfriend,' I explain. 'She hasn't done much sewing since school.'

'And these marks on your neck. They look like bites.'

'They are.'

'Also your girlfriend?'

'Uh-huh.'

'Well, I'm sure you know what you're doing. Be careful, OK.'

I knock on Oxana's door. When she answers she's damp from the shower and wrapped in a white bathrobe. With her spiky haircut and moist pink skin she looks almost childlike.

'Do you know anything about this place?' I ask her. 'Did Konstantin or anyone else ever mention it?'

'Never.'

112

The bedside telephone rings. Oxana answers it, listens for twenty seconds, and hangs up. 'That was Richard. He says we've all had a stressful day, ha fucking ha, and he'd like to invite us to meet for a quiet, informal dinner. He thinks we should all get to know each other better, so that we can draw a line under this morning's unfortunate events and move on.'

'Move on,' I say. 'Seriously? He's completely fucking insane.'

'Well I'm starving, so it's fine by me. Lara's coming to collect us in fifteen minutes. Wear the bee sweater. I like you in that.'

The twelfth floor is luxurious, in an impersonal, chain-hotel sort of way, but we are unquestionably prisoners. The triple-glazed windows can't be opened, and the exit door to the lift is code-controlled. Watchful young men and women, some of them carrying weapons, patrol the corridors and move between cryptically numbered offices. By the time we leave Oxana's room the place is as busy as ever. Their work, whatever it is, continues day and night.

Dinner is in a suite overlooking the river. The decor is Stalinist neoclassical with a twist, and we're shown to our places by suited waiters with a distinct paramilitary air. I'm seated between Lara and Anton, which presents an interesting conversational challenge, and Oxana is opposite me next to Richard. Oxana and I are both underdressed for our surroundings, but then we didn't exactly ask to be here.

'This is all deeply weird,' I say to Anton, and he shrugs.

'It's Russia,' he replies. 'A theatre where the play is rewritten every day. And the cast change roles mid-performance.'

'So what role are you playing right now?'

'A small but necessary one. A spear carrier. And what about you, Mrs Polastri?'

'Given that you've tried to have me killed three times now, I think you can probably call me Eve, don't you?'

'Very well.' He pauses as a waiter pours wine into his glass. 'So, Eve, may I ask you, how does it feel to be running with the hounds rather than the hare?'

'To be honest, I was hoping to avoid the hunt altogether.'

'Too late. You left that option behind you when you murdered Asmat Dzabrati.' He smiles. 'Yes, we know all about that.'

'I see.' The stitches in my back are throbbing angrily. The wound feels raw and jagged.

'You think you're different from the rest of us, Eve, but you're not.' He takes an exploratory sip of his wine. 'This is really good. Try some.'

'I'm afraid that if I drink so much as a drop, I'm going to pass out. It's been the most traumatic day of my life, starting with the moment when Lara shot Kristina dead, thinking that she was me.'

'That's exactly why you need a glass of this excellent Romanian Chardonnay.'

I touch the heavy crystal glass to my lips for politeness' sake, and take a deep, cold swallow. Anton's right, it's delicious.

'I wasn't always a soldier,' he continues. 'My first love was literature, especially Shakespeare, so I appreciate a moral dilemma. I'm not like your lady friend over there, devoid of feeling and thought.'

'You don't know her,' I say, surreptitiously necking a couple of painkillers with the wine.

'Oh but I do, Eve. I do know her. And I know exactly how she works. She's like a clockwork toy you can take apart and put back together over and over again. She's entirely predictable, which is what makes her so useful. Enjoy her all you want, but don't make the mistake of thinking she'll ever be human.'

I'm saved from replying by the arrival of the first course. 'Scallops from Okhotsk,' murmurs the waiter before slipping a porcelain plateful in front of me.

'Wow,' says Lara, squeezing a lemon segment over their scallops with such force that juice squirts in my eye. 'Oh fuck. Shit.' They dab at my face with their napkin. 'First that girl this morning and now this. It's not our day, is it?'

'How long have you been, um, gender non-binary?' I ask them.

Lara brightens. 'Since I was in England, a few months ago. Have you ever been to Chipping Norton?'

'Never. My loss, I'm sure.'

'I was an au pair there with a family. The Weadle-Smythes. I looked after their daughters. Fifteen-year-old twins.'

'How did that go?'

'It was really nice. The father was only there at weekends; he was a Conservative MP with a red face who spent almost all of his time in London. He had a girlfriend there, some sort of prostitute I think, but his wife didn't mind because it meant that she could sit up all night watching Netflix. And Celia and Emma were so sweet. They used to

115

take me out with them in the evening. We'd go to the local pub, get drunk, and then go dog-fighting.'

'Seriously?'

'Yes, they were a very traditional, upper-class family. The girls asked me if I had a boyfriend back in Russia, and obviously I said no. I explained that I worked in this quite macho world – I was vague about what I actually did – and I didn't think of myself as girly and feminine, and didn't like to be treated that way. So they said why didn't I change my pronouns, which was kind of funny since I was sent there to improve my English. So I did.'

'How did that go down with the parents?'

'The mother was like "why are you referring to Lara as 'they', girls? She hasn't split in two" and the father rolled his eyes and talked about the "PC Brigade", so yeah. And then suddenly I was called back here to Moscow to . . .' Their hand flies to their mouth. 'Shit, you won't believe it. I was going to say that I was called back to shoot some woman, but then I remembered that the woman was you.'

'Small world. And you missed.'

'You ducked.'

'Was that cheating?'

'You're so funny. Oxana always said I have no sense of humour.'

'I'm sure you have other wonderful qualities.' Watching them chomping the scallops, I'm reminded of Oxana's comment about their jaws.

'Yes, many. But we're quits now, yes? I tried to shoot you—'

'Twice.'

'OK, twice. But you took my girlfriend.'

'She was never yours, Lara, she was always mine.'

'That's not true.'

'Yes it is. Tell me more about the gender thing.'

'Yes, tell us about it,' says Anton, overhearing. 'What is all that about? I mean, you do a man's job, and nobody makes an issue about it, so what's the problem?'

'Why is shooting people with a rifle and telescopic sights a man's job?' asks Lara, spearing another scallop. 'Anyone can learn to do it. I'm fed up with being called a female sniper. I'm just a sniper. A *torpedo*. I don't want the bullshit that comes with people thinking of me as a woman.'

'Or the privileges?'

'What privileges? Men staring at my tits and talking to me like I'm stupid?'

'No one talks to you like you're stupid,' says Richard, who's been listening to these exchanges. 'People think you're clever because you have the best of both worlds. You're treated with respect as an elite assassin, and also admired as a very spectacular young woman.' He raises his glass to her with creepy gallantry.

Lara regards him doubtfully. 'You can say what you like, but my pronouns are my pronouns. If you don't use them I'm not shooting anyone. I'm going to change my name, too.'

'You're not becoming a vegetarian, are you?' asks Anton.

'Don't be ridiculous.'

The waiter announces the second course. My Russian vocabulary isn't wide when it comes to the larger mammals, but it's something like elk or reindeer. Something that once had antlers, and has now been reduced to dark, bloody steaks in a red berry sauce. Our glasses are exchanged for larger ones and charged with Georgian wine that's so easy to drink I need a refill almost immediately. On the other side of the table Oxana, animated by the morning's slaughter, is on sparkling form. She meets Richard's condescension with demure flirtatiousness, studiously ignores Anton, stares lasciviously at Lara, and shoots tender, soft-eyed glances at me. It's a performance, a chance to run through her repertoire of learnt responses.

When I was a teenager my parents had a cat, a beautiful, murderous creature called Violet, although Violent would have been a better name, who presented them daily with bloodied and dying voles, mice and small birds. I hated the sight of these heartbreaking little tributes, and begged my parents to put a bell on Violet, or give her more food at home, but they were having none of it. 'It's just how cats are,' they told me. 'It's instinctive. She needs to hunt.' Violet died as brutally as she'd lived, under the wheels of a speeding car at night, and looking back on the years she spent with us I think my parents not only tolerated their cat's savage ways, but were secretly gratified by them. Violet's behaviour was in some sense authentic and enabled them to feel superior to city folk who preferred to avert their eyes from nature's darker realities. I understand my parents better now. Oxana, red in tooth and claw, is my Violet. She is how the world is, when you look at it without blinking, or flinching. She needs to hunt.

Richard taps his glass with his knife, and I open my eyes. I'm so tired, so utterly exhausted, it's as much as I can do to stop myself sliding under the table. 'Can we all just stand up a moment and walk to the window?' Richard asks.

Lara helps me to my feet. They seem to believe that we're pals now.

118

Loosening his tie, Richard starts to talk. With an expansive sweep of his arm, he indicates the blazing expanse of the city. After the dilapidated grandeur of St Petersburg, Moscow is fortress-like and monolithic. It's impressive, but too inhuman in scale to be beautiful. I feel myself swaying. Lara steadies me with a hand on my arm.

'Everything that you see before you is dead or dying,' Richard says. 'Nothing works. There are no big political ideas, no great leaders, nothing to give people hope. I'm not just talking about Russia, but Russia is the perfect illustration of what I'm saying. Everything that people value, everything that once made them proud, belongs to the past. Communism was flawed as a system, but there was an ideal there, once upon a time. An aspiration. People understood that they were part of something, however imperfect. Now there is nothing. Nothing except the systematic looting of the nation's assets by a rapacious, self-appointed elite.'

His words have the sheen of frequent usage. He's spoken them before, perhaps many times. Oxana is listening with a slight frown on her face, Anton is expressionless, and Lara, who has let go of my arm, is examining their fingernails.

Sensing my eye on them, Lara inclines towards me. 'What do you think of the name Charlie?' they whisper. 'I really like it. Oxana was codenamed Charlie on the Odessa job and I was *super*-jealous.'

'It's nice. Suits you.'

'So what does the Twelve propose?' Richard continues, turning away from the window to face us. 'What have all our plans and strategies been leading up to? A new world, nothing less. We put the corrupt old men out of their misery, and we rebuild.'

'He likes to talk, doesn't he?' Lara murmurs.

'Mmm.'

'You really think Charlie suits me?'

'Uh-huh.'

'The old dies, the new is born. That's how history works. A golden age comes to pass – an era of prosperity, nobility and wisdom – and then over the course of millennia things decline until that golden age is just a folk memory, a set of half-understood stories, a vague longing for what has been lost. And that's where we are now. Feeling our way through the darkness.'

'Not Alex?'

'No. Charlie's perfect.'

'You're right. Everyone's called Alex.'

'But we can find it again, that golden age, because history is cyclic. All that is needed is a few good people. Men and women with the vision to see that the old must be destroyed to make way for the new, and the courage to do it.'

Richard's voice continues its urbane flow. I read somewhere that Etonians learn a skill called 'oiling', which is the art of courteously, but firmly, persuading others to your point of view. Richard is oiling us now, but his words are beginning to run together. I pull out my chair, and as I lower myself to the cushioned seat Oxana flicks an irritated glance at me. I'm not very drunk, but I feel heavy-limbed and uncoordinated. It's as much as I can do not to lie down under the dining table and close my eyes.

'And that, my friends, is where we come in,' Richard says. 'We are the advance guard of the new age. And we're not alone. All over the world there are people like ourselves, aristocrats of the spirit, waiting for the moment to strike.

But our task is perhaps the hardest, and the most dangerous. With one decisive action, we have to set the whole process in motion. And so I ask you all – Villanelle, Eve, Lara, and of course you Anton, old friend – are you with us? Are you ready to go down in history?'

Oxana nods.

Anton narrows his pale gaze. 'All the way.'

'Sure,' says Lara. 'But from now on it's Charlie. Lara is my deadname.'

Richard gives her the ghost of a bow. 'Very well, Charlie it is. Eve, you look . . . uncertain.'

'It's been a long day. But let me get this right. This morning you seemed quite anxious to end my life, and now you want me to join your team?'

'Why not? We could use your input. And correct me if I'm wrong, but I sense that you would welcome the challenge of a new world order. The old one didn't do a great deal for you, after all.'

'You're sure I'm not too . . . what was it you called me this morning? Ordinary?'

'Eve, we were all in a different place this morning. I think you're exceptional.'

I shrug. 'OK.'

As if I had the ghost of a choice.

Somehow, the meal draws to a close, and Oxana steers me back to her room. I can hardly place one foot in front of the other. Oxana's snoring within a couple of minutes, her arms out-thrown, her mouth wide open, but I'm so tired that I can't sleep. The stitches don't help. The painkillers and the wine have kicked in, reducing the pain to a hot, dull throb, but I still get a warning stab if I move too suddenly.

What have I agreed to? Is any one of us going to get out alive? From Richard's apocalyptic tone, and his talk of the danger of the mission, I would guess not. None of the foot soldiers, anyway. Richard himself, of course, is another matter. If one thing is certain it's that when the smoke clears he'll still be standing there, Old Etonian tie knotted, urbane smile in place.

And yet I said yes. Whatever the project involves, it must surely include the murder of at least one prominent figure. It seems strange that Richard should want me to be part of the team. He probably just wants me on board to keep Oxana happy, or as a way of controlling her.

It's weird. On the one hand I know that Richard's speech is brassy, echoing bullshit. That all this talk of golden ages and spiritual rebirth is just cover for what will undoubtedly turn out to be one more squalid political coup. On the other hand, there's something perversely thrilling about being locked into a conspiracy with Oxana. For all its horror, this is her world. I knew that when I abandoned my own. And was it really so ridiculous, Richard's talk of destruction and rebirth? Hadn't I done the same thing myself? Destroyed my old life to make way for my truer, darker self?

I turn over in bed at the same time as Oxana and we collide in a confusion of limbs.

'Go to sleep, stupid,' she murmurs blearily.

'I'm kind of terrified,' I tell her. 'And my back hurts.'

'I know.'

'They're going to kill us. They're just making us do one last job for them first.'

'Probably.'

'What do you mean, *probably*?'

The bedclothes shift as she raises herself on one elbow. 'I mean that you have to live in the present, *pchelka*. I've told you this before. Right now, we're fine, and we need to sleep. You especially. Tomorrow, when we've cleared our heads, we'll make a plan.'

'Aren't you afraid?'

'How do you mean? Of what?'

'Of everything that might happen.'

'No. I'm not afraid. We'll find out soon enough what they want from us, then we can figure out our next move. Right now they need us, and that's all that matters.'

I reach out in the dark and feel her face. The line of her cheek and her mouth. I touch her lips and she bites my finger. 'You're enjoying this,' I say. 'We're on this insane death ride, totally out of control, and . . .'

I feel her shrug. 'You know what I am. Read the textbooks. They'll tell you that people like me are very bad at processing threat.'

'Is that true?'

'No, it's bullshit. What's true is that we don't get fucked up. We stay calm and focused. We get our sleep, and we live to fight another day.'

'So you've read psychopathy textbooks?'

'Of course. All the so-called important ones. They're actually quite funny. All those creepy guys desperately trying to figure us out. You know, don't you, that all the case studies are male? They just assume that female psychopaths work the same way.'

'They get it wrong?'

'All the time.'

'Give me an example.'

She yawns. 'Like, for a start, they say psychopaths aren't capable of falling in love.'

'And are they?'

'Of course they are. I mean, I love you, baby bee.'

I can't speak. Oxana reaches out and I feel her hand close over my heart. 'Listen to you,' she says. 'Boom, boom, boom. You're so sweet.'

'Why didn't you say?'

'Why didn't *you* say, dumbass? You do love me, don't you?'

'I . . . yes, of course I do.'

'Well then, there we go. Now turn over, so that I can spoon into you, and go to sleep.'

Breakfast, by unspoken agreement, is conducted in near silence, the only sound in the dining room the murmur of the waiters as they dispense joltingly strong coffee. We all take the same places as the night before. Outside the snow flies past the windows, caught in the rogue currents surrounding the building. Looking out, as I pile my plate with scrambled eggs and salmon caviar, I can barely see the ground. Just the black sweep of the highway and the grey-green curve of the river.

Oxana chooses the same dishes as me and stares fixedly in front of her as she eats. She's in a wretched mood. When we woke up this morning, our bodies entwined, she extricated herself with fastidious distaste before dressing in a whirlwind fury. It was as if I revolted her, as if she couldn't bear to be naked in front of me. All that I can do is avoid her gaze and wish myself elsewhere.

I know what's going on. In saying that she loves me Oxana thinks she's gone too far, so she's trying to unsay it by hating me. And it's working. Charlie looks at us as if keen to talk, but on seeing our expressions turns away and starts carefully spreading themself successive squares of toast and apricot jam. Beside them, Anton devours soft, flaky pastries.

By the time Richard arrives we've all finished. Ignoring the food, he pours himself a cup of coffee, and takes his place at the table.

'We have ten days,' he announces. 'Ten days to prepare for an operation that will require supreme daring and technical skill. If we succeed – when we succeed – we change the course of history.' He spreads his hands and looks at each of us in turn. 'I want you all to remember the words of Field Marshal Suvorov, which I believe were much admired at your former regiment, Anton?'

'They were indeed,' Anton says. ' "Train hard, fight easy." Painted on the CO's door.'

'We'll be leaving midday tomorrow,' Richard continues. 'Destination to be announced in due course. Today is for supply and paperwork. We'll be measuring you up for clothes and equipment, and taking photographs for passports, etcetera. It's a tight turnaround, but our people are used to working against the clock. Your documents, clothes and hand luggage are being delivered in twenty-four hours. Your weaponry is waiting for you at the training destination.'

I listen with increasing disbelief. I agreed to be involved in whatever Richard and the Twelve are planning because of Oxana, and because I had no choice. I couldn't imagine Richard and Anton, knowing what they know about me, being so suicidally unwise as to award me any but the most minor, walk-on role. A couple of days on the range at Bullington doesn't add up to any kind of real training. I can fire, dismantle and clean a Service-issue Glock, but that's as far as it goes. I've spent my professional life behind a desk. I wear glasses. What part could I possibly play in an operation requiring 'supreme daring and technical skill'? I'd be a liability, and it would be crazy to think otherwise. Yet Richard is clearly including me in this briefing.

The day passes slowly and miserably. Oxana is unreachable, she won't even look at me. Instead she flirts listlessly with Charlie, making sure that I can see, and stares out the windows. With its stale, climate-controlled atmosphere, the apartment is oppressive. Everyone is on edge. The snow continues to fall all day, and although it's freezing on the streets I'd give anything to be out there, breathing the clean, cold air. Impossible, of course. We can't even open a window.

Dinner is once again superlative but I have no appetite, and the smell of rare meat and blood-thickened gravy turns my stomach. Instead, that evening, I drink the best part of a bottle of Château Pétrus, a wine so expensive that I never thought I'd taste it. Seeing me pouring my fifth glass, Richard looks at me indulgently. 'Pétrus is the unofficial house wine of the Twelve,' he says. 'You're going to fit in perfectly.'

'I'm definitely looking forward to drinking a shitload of this stuff,' I say, hearing my voice slur. 'Assuming I make it back alive, that is.'

'Oh you will,' he replies. 'You're very hard to kill. It's one of the things I like most about you.'

'You don't like anything about me,' I say, swaying aggressively towards him and spilling a crimson splash of wine on the damask tablecloth. 'You just need me because you need my girlfriend. Cheers.'

He smiles. 'But is she? Your girlfriend, I mean. She seems to be getting on very well with Lara, or whatever she's calling herself these days.'

I see what he means. On the other side of the table, Oxana is playing with Charlie's hand, holding their gaze and nipping their fingertips between her teeth.

'If that was her trigger finger I'd be worried,' Richard says, but I'm already out of my chair and moving unsteadily round the table.

'I need a word,' I say to Oxana.

'Maybe she's busy.'

'Fuck off, Charlie. Oxana, you heard me.'

She follows me. More out of curiosity, I'm guessing, than anything else.

Slamming the bedroom door behind me I slap Oxana's face so hard that, for a moment, she's shocked into wide-eyed immobility. 'Enough, OK? Enough of your stupid sulking, enough of this shit with Charlie, enough of you being such a complete and utter bitch.'

My hand stings and it feels like the stitches in my back have torn open. Oxana recovers herself and flicks me a sly half-smile. 'You knew what you were getting into with me. You knew better than anyone.'

'Fuck you, Oxana. That's not good enough. You can't go through your life saying I am what I am and that's the end of it. You're worth more than that. We're worth more than that.'

'Really? Well perhaps I like how I am. Perhaps I don't want to be what you want me to be, has that thought ever crossed your mind?'

127

'Yes, every day. Every single day since—'

'Since you gave up everything to be with me? Are you going to drag that one out again? Because I tell you, Polastri, it's not very fucking sexy, OK?'

'Whatever. I really don't care any more.'

'Oh boohoo, you pussy.'

Walking over to the window, I look down at the figures on the pavement below, braced against the driving snow. 'Listen to me,' I tell her. 'The only reason I'm here, the only reason I'm even alive, is that Richard and Anton think that you care what happens to me. They need you, so they keep me around. But you know what? I think I'd rather tell them that they're wrong, that you don't actually give a shit about me. Then they can just put a bullet through the back of my head and get it over with. I've had enough.'

'Eve, I never said I didn't care about you. Last night—'

'What about last night?'

'You heard what I said.'

'You said you loved me.'

'I meant it.'

'And then you panicked. You thought you'd given me something, some kind of power, that I'd use against you. You didn't trust me to love you back, so you turned on me, like you always do.'

'You've thought it all out, haven't you? Got all the theories. But you know something? That doesn't make you someone who cares. It just makes you the latest in a long line of assholes who've been poking at my mind ever since I was a child.'

'I'm just trying to understand you.'

128

'Don't. You understood me better before you met me, when I was just the worst fucking person you could imagine. A monster you had to hunt down. Think of me like that and you won't go far wrong.'

I turn round to face her. 'Oxana.'

'What?'

'We have one more night here. Two at the most. Then God knows what.' I walk towards her, and place my hands on her arms. Her muscles twitch through her thin sweater, and her depthless grey eyes hold mine. I touch a finger to the ridge of scar tissue on her lip and hear the faint shiver of her breath. 'Like you said, now's all there is. And you're all that I have and all that I want.'

She frowns, as if trying to recall a distant memory. 'I don't feel all the things that other people do. I have to fake some of them. But I do have my own kind of love. It's probably not the same as . . .' She shrugs faintly. 'But it's real.'

'I know it is.'

She looks away and I catch the flash of tears. I taste them when I kiss her.

'I'm sorry,' she says. 'I'm a mess. Just fuck me, OK?'

# 8

The clothes arrive the next morning. Boxes of weather-proof jackets and parkas, winter hats, trousers, thermal underwear and boots. None of it ostentatious, but all designer-branded and clearly expensive. Then a cabin suit-case for each of us, and folders containing used Russian international passports, driving licences, credit cards and other identifying papers in the same names.

'Where do you think we're going?' Charlie asks me.

'Hawaii?'

We leave at midday, and as we step out of the lift in our designer outfits and follow Richard through the building's endless succession of lobbies, no one gives us a second glance. We could be an upscale tour-group, or prosperous Russians setting off on holiday. Outside, it's wonderfully cold, and I turn into the wind for a moment so that the snowflakes fly into my face. Then, all too soon, we're climbing into a Porsche SUV with dark-tinted windows. Anton drives, Richard takes the front seat, and I sit between Oxana and Charlie.

We drive north-west, following the signs to Sheremetyevo airport. Visibility is limited, and the road surface treacherous. The outlines of broken-down vehicles are visible on the hard shoulder, hazard lights winking. I'm nervous, but glad that Oxana is at my side. I'm even glad, in a perverse sort of way, that Charlie's there.

We're crossing the outer ring road when a police vehicle swings in front of us, blue lights flashing. 'Fuck's sake,' Anton mutters, bringing the Porsche to a halt in the slush. 'What now?'

There's a sharp tap on the passenger-side window and Richard lowers it. The features of the uniformed figure outside are obscured by his helmet and face mask, but his shoulder patch identifies him as an officer of the FSB, Russia's internal security service. Ahead of us, other vehicles similar to ours have been stopped. Several drivers and passengers have been ordered out of their cars and directed, documents in hand, to an armoured truck with iron-grille windows and FSB insignia, parked on the side of the highway.

'What's going on, Lieutenant?' Richard asks the officer, as wind and snow blast into the Porsche's interior.

'Security check. Passports please?'

We hand them over, he checks them carefully, and peers at us one by one through the passenger window. Then he returns all the passports except mine. 'Out please,' he tells me, pointing to the truck with a gloved hand.

It's freezing outside, and I pull the hood of my parka over my head as I join the line outside the truck. 'Must be looking for someone important,' I say to the woman in front of me, a grandmotherly figure in a pink woollen headscarf.

She shrugs, indifferent, and stamps her booted feet in the snow. 'They're always looking for someone. They just stop cars at random.'

132

Eventually, it's my turn. I climb the steps into the truck, and when I get inside stand for a few seconds, eyes narrowed. It's dark in there after the snow-brightness. Two officers are sitting on metal benches opposite me, and one is in the shadows to my left. At a signal from the man in the shadows the others leave.

'Mrs Polastri. Eve. I'm so glad that the reports of your death were exaggerated.'

I recognise the voice, and when he moves into one of the shafts of light admitted by the iron-grille windows, I recognise the man. Broad shoulders made broader by a military greatcoat, buzz-cut silver hair, a wry smile.

'Mr Tikhomirov. This is a surprise. And yes, it's good to be alive.'

'I saw the photograph. It was good, and would have fooled most people but . . . what do they say? Don't bullshit a bullshitter. In our world, as you know, nothing is what it looks like, even life and death. Everything's a simulacrum.'

Vadim Tikhomirov is a senior officer of the FSB. A general, in fact, although he's not the kind of man to advertise his rank. We first met in complicated circumstances after Charlie – or Lara as they were then – tried and failed to shoot me in the VDNKh Metro station in Moscow. On that occasion Tikhomirov not only got me out of Russia, he discreetly alerted me to the fact that my boss, Richard Edwards, was an asset of the Twelve.

Tikhomirov is the refined face of an often brutally uncompromising organisation, and where his own loyalties lie I'm not sure. Is he, as he appears to be, a dedicated servant of the Russian state, and if so, what does that actually entail? Unquestioning obedience to the diktats of the Kremlin, or the playing of longer, more ambiguous games?

He leans towards me on the bench. 'Eve, we have very little time. If we don't keep this short your friends outside are going to be suspicious. Firstly, you've done brilliantly to insert yourself into a Twelve operation.'

I stare at him. Does he really think that's why I'm here? That I'm still working for MI6?

'How do I know this? Let's just say that we have a friend in common in St Petersburg. But it's imperative that we discover what the Twelve are planning, because if what I suspect is true the consequences will be catastrophic, and not just for Russia. So you absolutely have to find out, Eve. And you have to tell me.'

It's as cold as a butcher's fridge in the truck, and I zip my jacket up to the chin.

'You know who's in that Porsche SUV, don't you? Our mutual friend Richard Edwards. Why don't you just arrest him?'

'Nothing I'd rather do, believe me. But I can't. I have to let him run. See who he leads us to.'

'Isn't that a bit risky? I mean—'

'This is the Twelve we're dealing with, Eve. We need to take down the whole organisation, and if we're going to do that we need to aim a lot higher than Edwards. He's useful to them but he's replaceable, and probably doesn't know that much anyway.'

'I see.' This is not sounding good.

'So, we need to keep our nerve, let them think it's safe to go ahead, and wait for the key players to reveal themselves. Then, and only then, can we make our move. First we have to know what they've been planning.'

'And that's where I come in?'

'Exactly.'

'So tell me.'

'I'm going to give you a phone number, which you're going to memorise, and the rest is up to you. You're a highly resourceful individual, and I'm confident that one way or another you'll succeed.' He lets his words hang in the air. 'So are you with me? I'm afraid that you have to decide right here, right now.'

'One condition.'

'Tell me.'

'Oxana Vorontsova.'

'Ah. The famous Villanelle. I thought we might get to her.'

'Don't kill her. Please, I . . .' I stare at him helplessly.

He meets my gaze, his eyes thoughtful, and then turns to the door. Slowly, barely perceptibly, he nods his head. 'I can guarantee nothing. I have to consider the optics. But if you do this thing for me I will try to do this for you. Here is the number . . .'

He says it three times. Makes me repeat it three times.

'They've taken our guns, phones, pens, everything,' I tell him. 'They'll be watching us all the time. I don't know how I'm going to—'

'You'll find a way, Eve. I know you will.' He stands up, bowing his head beneath the low roof of the truck. 'And now you have to go.'

As I stand in my turn, a handsome young man in a winter camouflage uniform climbs into the truck, and I recognise Dima, Tikhomirov's assistant. A long look passes between them.

'Please,' I whisper. 'Remember.'

Tikhomirov looks at me, his expression sad, and raises his hand.

As I trudge back to the SUV, I repeat the number he gave me.

'So what did they want?' Richard asks, when we're back on the motorway.

'They checked my appearance against a set of photographs of women that they had on a laptop. I didn't look anything like any of the photographs – all the women were wearing black Islamic headscarves – and the officers didn't ask my name. I asked them what it was all about but they wouldn't tell me.'

'So who was there?'

'An FSB officer, in his forties probably, and two junior guys. A fourth guy came in from having a cigarette just as I left. I didn't get the impression they were very interested in what they were doing.'

'They didn't photograph you? Take your fingerprints? Take a copy of your passport?'

'Nothing like that, no.'

Anton looks back at me and grins. 'Just checking out women to pass the time?'

'Probably.'

Richard leaves us on the tarmac at Sheremetyevo airport, beneath a bruise-dark sky. He shakes our hands through the driver's window of the Porsche, and gives us each a taut, crinkle-eyed smile that doesn't quite mask his relief that he's not coming with us. How did I work for him for so long without spotting that phoney manner?

The Learjet lifts off shortly afterwards, heading west-wards. Our immediate destination, Anton tells us, is Ostend, in Belgium. No one enquires further.

Oxana sits next to me, her head on my shoulder, and we talk about the things we'll do, and the places we'll visit, when all of this is over. We both know it's a fantasy, that we'll probably never walk hand in hand by the River Neva in St Petersburg, watching the ice-floes drift past, or sit in the sun on a spring morning in the courtyard of Oxana's favourite café in Paris, but we promise ourselves these things and more. I say nothing about my conversation with Tikhomirov. I try not to think about it at all, and to ignore the ghastly sensation that we are sleepwalking towards a cliff edge. Instead, I lose myself in the moment, feeling the soft weight of Oxana's head on my shoulder.

After three and a half hours we land at Ostend–Bruges airport. The light has almost gone, and as we leave the warmly upholstered interior of the Learjet we're met with a bitter wind and driving sleet. A minibus is waiting for us on the tarmac, and we're driven a few hundred metres to a waiting Super Puma helicopter, where the pilot hands us noise-cancelling headsets. The helicopter's rotors are already swinging as we board, and the lights of the airport vanish behind us as we gain height over desolate beaches and the wind-blurred expanse of the North Sea.

Oxana tucks in next to me again, but with the engine noise and the headsets conversation is impossible. Where we're going, I have no idea, although Oxana's pensive expression suggests that she may have figured it out. We hold a roughly north-western course towards England, but why would we be travelling there by helicopter? If our destination is London, we could have flown there directly from Moscow. Are we going to be landing on a ship?

After forty-five minutes we start our descent. The helicopter's spotlights illuminate dark, wrinkling waves. 'We're there,' Oxana mouths at me. 'Look.' She jabs a finger downwards.

At first I see only the surface of the sea. Then a grey rectangle swings into view, and the Super Puma's spotlights lock on to it. A marine platform, its size hard to estimate, supported by two trunk-like columns. As we approach the platform I see that there's a helipad at one end, which two tiny human figures are illuminating with torches. Never in my life have I seen anything so unforgivingly harsh. 'Fucking hell,' I mouth at Oxana, and she nods.

We touch down, and the Super Puma rests on the helipad for no more than thirty seconds as we climb out into the bitter, sleeting wind. It's so ferocious, I'm afraid that if I lose my footing I'll be swept away, and I cling to the arm of the nearest person, who happens to be Anton. He shouts something to me, but it's whipped away in the wind.

We walk the length of the platform, heads down, to where three converted shipping containers are lashed to the decking with steel hawsers. Anton guides us inside the nearest of these, flicks on an electric light, and when we're all inside, including the two men who guided in the helicopter, closes the steel door.

It's not much, but it's a lot more homely than the last container I was in. Two double-glazed windows have been let in to the lengthways wall, framing views of the sea and the sky. At one end there's a trestle table and six folding chairs, at the other a microwave, a chest freezer, and a kettle. A tray on the table holds jars of honey, Marmite, and strawberry jam. Above it, there's a bookshelf stocked with well-thumbed paperback thrillers by Mick Herron, Andrei Kivinov, and others, and a hardback copy of Mangan and Proctor's *Birds of the North Sea*.

'Welcome to Knock Tom,' Anton says. 'It was originally a Second World War anti-aircraft emplacement, built by the British to protect the North Sea shipping lanes. So if you get bored and feel like a swim' – he points out of the further window – 'the Essex coast is about ten miles in that direction. But I promise that you won't be bored. We've got a lot of work to do and a lot of ground to cover.

'So let's get to it. First off, meet Nobby and Ginge. They are going to be your instructors and your watchdogs, so listen up and do what they say. They're former E Squadron sniper team leaders, so they know their stuff. Lara and Villanelle, I know you have experience as solo operatives, but this project poses unique challenges. Our targets, plural, have the best security the world has to offer. Teamwork is going to be vital.'

'Charlie. My name is Charlie. Since you're talking about teamwork.'

Silence. Nobby and Ginge exchange grins.

Anton looks as if he's swallowed a wasp. 'Charlie it is, then. Moving on. We're going to be using two teams, each with a spotter and a shooter. The window of opportunity will be small, and the weather conditions challenging, so the role of the spotters will be critical. Our shooters will be Villanelle and, er, Charlie. Spotters will be Eve and myself.'

'So what's wrong with these two heroes?' Oxana asks, jerking a thumb at the two instructors. 'If they're so fucking experienced, how come you need us?'

Anton regards her with calm loathing. 'Nobby and Ginge have retired from the stage. They prefer to pass on their wisdom to a new generation.'

'It's that dangerous, then,' Oxana says and smirks.

'I'm not going to pretend it's not dangerous. It's very dangerous indeed. That's why preparation is everything. We have a week in which we can concentrate fully on the task at hand. There's no WiFi here, so you'll have no active links to the outside world. We are going to be living and breathing our mission. Train hard, fight easy.'

It's at this point that I lose hope. There's no way to contact Tikhomirov, and as I have no clue as to the identity of the target, or targets, there's no point in thinking about how to do so. Anton, moreover, clearly has no intention of telling us the details of the hit until the absolute last moment. Maybe he doesn't even know them. The fact that we have been flown all the way to the middle of the North Sea, rather than to a secure facility in Russia, tells me how concerned the Twelve are that no word of this operation should get out. We're confined to this tiny, isolated, storm-battered platform with no possibility of escape, and no way of contacting the outside world.

'The two teams will be training separately,' Anton continues. 'Villanelle and I with Nobby, Charlie and Eve with Ginge. Neither team will discuss the details of their mission with the other team. You all have separate quarters, three in the north leg of the platform, three in the south, and there will be no doubling up.' He looks balefully from me to Oxana. 'This is not a request, it's an order.'

Watching Anton, with his too-pale eyes, wolfish jaw and thin, fastidious mouth, I can't suppress a shiver. He's one of those men whose hatred of women is so deep, so central to his being, that it almost defines him. He knows where he stands with men. With Richard he's subtly obsequious; with Nobby and Ginge matey but superior. He's pretty sure where he stands with me, too, as I'm too much of a scaredy-cat to give him much trouble. But he has no idea how to deal with Charlie and Oxana, who are every bit as hard core as he is, and not frightened to let him know it. I turn to Oxana but she is staring expressionlessly into space. Impossible to tell what she thinks of the sleeping arrangements.

This briefing is followed by a meal of warm baked beans and luncheon meat prepared by Nobby, during which Oxana remains wordless and withdrawn, refusing to meet my eye. As hurtful as this is, it no longer surprises me. I'm familiar with her mood-cycle. I know that when I say good night to her, she will look straight through me, and she does.

My quarters, accessed by a vertical ladder from the deck, are a concrete-walled cabin in the interior of the north leg. Inside is a metal bunk bed furnished with a mattress, sheet and blanket, all damp to the touch, and a locker containing cold-weather combat clothes.

I'm bracing myself for the chilly business of undressing when there's a bang on the steel door. It's Charlie.

'So we're a team,' they say.

'Looks like it.' I sit down on my bunk, loosen my boots and kick them off. 'How's your cabin?'

'Same as yours, but I'm in the south leg, between Oxana and Nobby. Bit like being back in Butyrka.'

'I'm sorry you're stuck with me as your spotter. I have no idea what I'm supposed to do.'

'Are you good at mathematics?'

'Hopeless.'

'Because the spotter has to make all the calculations. You know: range, wind-direction, all that. And you have to keep us safe. You're the lookout.'

'Er, right. And you?'

'I'm looking through the rifle scope. That's all I see, that little circle. Until I take the shot. Then we get out of there, fast. Who do you reckon the target is?'

'I don't know, Charlie. I don't even want to think about it.'

'Not you, anyway. Makes a change.'

'Yes, there is that.'

Charlie leans against the rust-streaked wall, arms folded. 'Do you miss her? Oxana, I mean? When you're not with her?'

'Mmm. Yeah, I do. A lot. What was it like in prison?'

'Really shitty. Lonely. Bad sex.'

'Oh God, Charlie.'

'I know. But I thought I was going to be there for ever. So I was like in heaven when I learnt that I was going to get out. I mean, people say the Twelve are a patriarchal organi-sation, but I think they offer real opportunities for women and gender non-binary people. The chance to grow as a person and live your dream. Which for me has always been shooting people.'

'Dangerous work.'

'And I'm really good at it. I know you think I'm not, but—'

'I never said that.'

'You didn't need to. Listen, I know you're not impressed that I missed you twice, but maybe the whole situation had got too personal? Like I knew that Oxana liked you, or whatever, and that made me tense up? I have feelings too, you know. I'm not just some replicant, like Rachael in *Blade Runner*.'

'I know, Charlie.'

'But explain to me, why are you with a woman at all? I mean, you were married, weren't you? To that Niko guy? Oxana always called him the Polish asshole.'

'He wasn't an asshole, he was a good man, but yeah.'

'And that was OK?'

'Mmm. It was.'

'So what happened? Did you just wake up one morning and say fuck this shit, I want some pussy?'

'No, it wasn't like that.'

'So how was it, Eve? Tell me.'

'I think . . . God, it's so difficult. OK, to start with, Oxana – she was Villanelle then – just really fascinated me. I was stuck in this quite frustrating job, which I felt was going nowhere, and then suddenly here was this person who didn't obey any of the rules, who made life up as she went along, and did whatever the fuck she wanted and got away with it, and to begin with that made me kind of angry, because my own life was so . . . not like that. I thought, how dare she? I was kind of outraged by her. And then, little by little, I began to admire her skill, and her cunning, and the whole game she was playing. It was so personal. So intimate. You remember that bracelet she bought me in Venice?'

'Yes I remember the bracelet. I was super-pissed off with her about that.'

'I know. And at that point I hadn't even met her.'

'So get to the sex.'

'It wasn't really about the sex. Then.'

'It's always about the sex.'

'So why do you want to know?'

'Because I'm fucking jealous, Eve. Because I want her back.'

'Charlie, get real. Do you think any of us are going to walk away from this? That there's going to be some kind of happy-ever-after?'

'Don't you?'

'No. If we fail, we're dead. If we succeed, and the target's as high profile as they say it is, then we're dead too, because they're certainly not going to want us around to tell our story.'

'But why would any of us say anything? I wouldn't, you wouldn't, and Oxana definitely wouldn't. We'd just go on working for the Twelve.'

'Charlie, if the FSB heard so much as a whisper that any of us was involved, they'd have us in an interrogation cell in Lefortovo before you could say Baileys Irish Cream. And then we'd talk, trust me. Any one of us would talk.'

'I love Baileys, it's the best drink there is. And I'm sorry, but I want Oxana back. I mean, what have you and her got in common? Nothing. And this evening. She didn't even talk to you. You're not enough for her, Eve.'

'Go to bed, Charlie, I'm tired. I'll see you tomorrow.'

\*

I wake up early, and clamber down the ladder to the wash-room, or 'head' as Anton insists on calling it. It's tiny but it's private, and there's a freshwater shower heated by a generator. I try very hard to enjoy the sixty-odd seconds of steaming hot water I allow myself. I suspect I'm going to spend most of the day feeling very cold indeed.

At breakfast – tea, bacon sandwiches – I team up with Charlie and Ginge, a stocky, balding Welshman with a twinkling smile. 'Lovely day for it,' he grins, as the wind screams across the platform deck outside. He leads us to one end of the deck, where two makeshift hides, about ten metres apart, have been constructed from oil drums and tarpaulin. On the ground beneath the tarpaulin is a low mattress, and on the mattress is a sniper rifle with scope attachment, a metal ammunition box, and a water-proof rucksack. The edge of the platform is no more than two metres in front of us. Far below, the sea churns and boils, dashing itself against the platform's concrete legs.

'Right now, let's get comfy. You're on the gun, Charlie-girl. Eve, you're behind and to the right, and I'll just tuck in on the left. Proper cosy, isn't it?'

I see Charlie tense up at being called a girl, and then deliberately relax. We settle into our places on the mattress. It's weird to be quite so close to Ginge and Charlie, but a relief to be out of the wind. It's still very cold, though, and my back aches badly. Will I survive long enough to have the stitches taken out?

Ginge grins at Charlie. 'Gather you've done a bit of sniper-work before, then?'

'Some,' Charlie answers warily.

145

'In that case you'll probably know a lot of what I've got to tell you, but listen up anyway. This job is going to be a very tricky one. I'm not aware of the location of the firing point, or the identity of the target. But I do know that the window of opportunity is going to be very small, probably just seconds, the target will be moving, and the range will be in excess of seven hundred metres. So Charlie, you are going to have to act very fast and very decisively, while remaining very calm. Eve, your job is to make sure that she can do that.

'So first, your weapon. It's a British-made AX sniper rifle with a Nightforce scope. The rifle's light, it's smooth-firing and it's very accurate. Altogether a tidy piece of kit.' He opens the ammunition box to reveal rows of shining, brass-cased cartridges. 'Calibre is .338 Lapua Magnum. High power. Send one of these your target's way and he's a mess. So, Charlie, what would you normally take into account when lining up a five-hundred-metre-plus shot?'

Charlie frowns. 'Range, wind force and direction, drag, spin-drift, Coriolis . . .'

Ginge gives me an evil smile. 'This making any sense to you, Eve?'

'Not a lot.'

'Don't worry, it will do. Let's start with range. The further a projectile has to travel, the more it drops in the air due to gravity, OK?'

'Got it.'

'Wind is also a factor. A strong crosswind will take a bullet off-course laterally, and a headwind will add drag. Cold air is denser than hot air, so that increases drag as well.'

146

'Right.'

'A bullet leaves the barrel of a rifle spinning at very high speed. This causes a very slight drift towards the direction of twist, which needs to be compensated for at long ranges.'

'Er, OK. I think I basically get that. And the other thing?'

'Want to talk us through the Coriolis effect, Charlie?'

'Sure. Say I shoot at Eve, right?'

'Again?'

They smile.

'Say I shoot at you at a range of a kilometre, the bullet's going to be in the air for three or four seconds before it hits you, OK?'

'I guess.'

'So while the bullet's in the air the earth continues to spin. And you're on the earth. So even if you don't move, you move. Get it?'

'Um . . . sort of. Yeah.'

'Righto then.' Ginge twinkles at me. I'm guessing that as a Special Forces sniper, working with Anton, he took out human targets with exactly the same merry smile on his face. 'In the old days, when I was in the game, we had to calculate all of these variables and adjust our sights accordingly. Fine if time was on your side, but awkward if it wasn't. Today we've got a laser system that makes all these calculations automatically. You just look through the scope, and there's your corrected aiming point.'

'So what am I here for?' I ask him.

'We'll get to that. First, let's set the rifle up. Charlie-girl, would you like to do the honours?'

'It's Charlie. Not Charlie-girl.'

'Is that right?' The smile never falters. 'Charlie it is, then.'

I've never thought of them as a particularly dextrous person, but watching Charlie calmly set the rifle on its bipod, fit their face to the cheekpiece, check the scope and work the bolt, I know immediately that I'm watching someone who's very, very good at what they do. As I watch, the weapon becomes an extension of their body.

'Eve, you get a lovely piece of kit too.' Ginge opens the waterproof rucksack and takes out an object like a truncated telescope. 'This is a Leupold spotting scope, for keeping eyes on the target. It's got much more powerful magnification than the telescopic sights on the rifle, so you can actually see, close up, where the sniper's shot goes.'

'Cool.'

'So I'll tell you what we're going to do next. If you look out to sea, about one o'clock, you should be able to see a red buoy. It's quite small and near the limit of visibility. Got it?'

I squint through my glasses, which have become blurry in the damp salt air, and finally see a tiny dot of red.

'Once you've got eyes on it,' Ginge orders us, 'look at it through your scopes.'

He's right, the Leupold is an amazing piece of kit. The buoy looks close enough to reach out and touch, as it swings from side to side on the waves.

'OK. That buoy is five hundred metres from this firing point, give or take, and that's the range we're going to be looking at today. I understand that the shot you're going to have to make on the day is at a range of just over seven hundred metres. Your target will be moving and the atmospherics will be challenging. So, shall we get to it?'

As Charlie and I rehearse the spoken procedure, Ginge sets up the targets. In the rucksack there's a box of yellow party balloons, a ball of twine, scissors, a bag of small plumb-weights, and an air canister. Ginge inflates a balloon, ties it off with a length of twine, attaches a weight and slings the whole thing off the edge of the platform. A minute later it drifts into view, blown by the wind towards the buoy. Ginge, meanwhile, is preparing the next balloon.

I let the first one drift for about a hundred metres, then pick it up in the spotter scope. The waves are not high, perhaps half a metre, but the rise and fall of the water is quite enough to make the balloon a hard target. At moments it disappears altogether. Beside me Charlie seems to draw into themself, and becomes almost preternaturally still. Cheek to cheekpiece, eye to eyepiece, finger to trigger.

'Range four eighty,' I announce. 'Four ninety. Send it.'

There's a sharp crack, instantly whipped away on the wind. The balloon continues its dance on the waves.

'Where did it go?' Ginge asks.

'I didn't see,' I confess. 'There wasn't a splash.'

'Don't look for the splash, watch the passage of the bullet. You should be able to follow the trace through the scope.'

Charlie fires again, and this time I see it. A tiny, transparent trail, spearing through the crosswind.

'One click to the right,' I tell Charlie.

A third crack, and the balloon disappears. I lift my eye from the scope and glimpse a pink balloon bobbing up and down a few metres to the left. There's a faint snapping sound and it vanishes.

'Looks like we've got competition,' murmurs Ginge. 'Anton reckons that other girlie's a real dead-eye. One of the best shots he's ever worked with.'

'Let's see,' says Charlie grimly, and Ginge gives me a wink.

As the hours slip by, we settle into an efficient routine. Charlie maintains a kind of zen state, their breathing slow, their cheek welded to the cheekpiece, their features wiped of expression. There's just the wind, the snapping of the frayed edge of the tarpaulin, and the quiet glide of the bolt. 'Send it,' I say, and wait for the whipped-away crack of the shot. I try not to think what we're preparing for. A .338 round is a hefty projectile and at a range of half a kilometre an upper body shot will leave an exit wound the size of a rabbit-hole. It's not quite the same thing as popping a balloon.

We continue to pop them, nevertheless, and so do Oxana and Anton. Ginge starts counting off our hits against theirs, yellow against pink, but there's really nothing in it. At midday we make our way to the canteen for tea and microwaved shepherd's pie, which we eat with plastic spoons. Oxana doesn't speak to me at lunch, or even look in my direction. Instead she hunkers down in her chair next to Anton, eating swiftly and in glowering silence. Nobby and Ginge sit together with their backs to me, comparing notes in an audible undertone. 'Yours might be more of a natural marksman,' Ginge murmurs. 'But long-term I'd back mine. She's—'

'You're not supposed to call her "she".'

'Bloody hell, I'm not, am I? But you just did.'

'Did what?'

'Call her "her".'

'Call who her?'

'Her. My one.'

'You wouldn't think they'd care, would you? Being Russian and that.'

'"They" as in both of them, or one of them?'

'Fuck knows. This PC lingo does my head in.'

'You're a dinosaur, boyo, that's your trouble. You should be woke, like me.'

'Ginge, no offence, mate, but you're basically a dwarf. Have you ever thought of doing porn?'

I sip a cup of tepid tea. I no longer have any idea what I'm doing, or why. Am I training to take part in a political assassination for the Twelve, or working as an undercover agent for Tikhomirov and the FSB? My compass is spinning. The only real allegiance I have is to Oxana. I'm rehearsing a murder to be at her side, and right now she won't even look at me.

But then, this is how Oxana is. Loving her is a kind of death. I feel hollowed out, as if the core of my being has been eaten away, like an apple by wasps. Is this what she always wanted? To occupy and toxify me? To make me wholly, helplessly hers, and then simply detach herself?

Ginge, Charlie and I return to the firing point, and continue until dark. The wind gets angrier as the light goes, and the desolation of the place seeps into my soul, or what's left of it. Charlie, meanwhile, is calm, patiently sending bullets to targets as I call the shots. I learn how to choose the moment to speak, how to align my breathing with Charlie's so that they're exhaling as the balloon is lifted by the swell, and squeezing off the shot as it achieves a

151

millisecond of stillness at the peak of the wave. For all the differences between us, we're a good team.

That night, as Nobby and Ginge exchange banter over the food preparation – impossible to call it cooking – and Oxana and I studiously ignore each other, Anton informs us that it's Christmas Day. Pulling a litre bottle of brandy and six paper cups from a locker, he pours a large shot into each and hands them out.

We look at each other awkwardly. Oxana bolts her brandy straight down and holds out her cup for more, which Anton hesitantly gives her. She knocks that back too, and retreats into sullen silence.

Charlie sips their brandy and shudders.

'Don't you like it?' I ask.

'I like it with hot chocolate, fifty-fifty. That's how Emma and Celia used to drink it. By itself it's too acid.'

'You're very good on that gun.'

'I know.' They look at me earnestly. 'But it's super-helpful for me, having you spotting. At the moment it's all just sea out there. But when we get to the real firing point you'll see how important your job is. Do you like working with me?'

The question takes me by surprise. For all Charlie's lethal proficiency, they can be almost childlike at moments. I'm about to answer when Oxana starts to dance. We all watch in amazement as she bops around the tiny space, winding between us with her arms and hips swaying. 'Come on, everyone,' she sings out. 'It's Christmas.'

No one moves. Instead they watch open-mouthed as Oxana throws open the steel door of the container and shimmies outside. After a moment I follow her onto the unlit platform deck, where she's still flailing around, her combat clothes flattened to her body by the salt wind. I grab her, terrified she's going to go too close to the edge, and she twists violently in my arms.

'Oxana, stop. Please.'

She starts to speak, but I have to put my ear to her mouth to hear her words against the roar of the gale. 'Didn't you hear what Anton said? It's Christmas.'

'I heard him, yes.'

'So don't you want to dance with me?'

'Not here.' I drag her back towards the door. 'Come inside.'

'Why won't you dance with me?' She stares at me accusingly. 'You're so fucking . . . *boring*.' She screams the word at me but it's plucked away on the wind.

I leave her there, her eyes streaming, her hair a crown of spikes around her face. Back in the container, the ping of the microwave announces that the food's ready. It's some kind of curry-based sludge from a packet. I help myself to a portion, but I'm so pissed off that I barely taste it.

Oxana comes back inside. Ignoring everyone, she takes a disproportionally large helping for herself, and starts shovelling it into her mouth. Her plastic spoon breaks almost immediately, so she throws the pieces on the floor and uses her hands.

There's a moment's silence, then Nobby launches into an anecdote about a woman he met in a club in Brentwood High Street and Charlie starts telling me how they're sure they have a future as a Hollywood film actor, and what do I think, and I pull myself together and say that stranger things have happened.

Physically, Charlie would make a good superhero, with their broad, sculpted features, muscled arms and statuesque body. And it may well be that audiences would overlook the homicide charge, the jail time, and the bizarre English accent. The problem, I suspect, would be the actual acting. Subtlety is not Charlie's forte. Witness the way that they're staring with frank, open-mouthed lust at Oxana, who's licking the last of the curry sauce from her paper plate.

'Charlie,' I say. 'It's not going to happen.'

Their gaze doesn't flicker. 'You really don't know her at all, do you?'

The next morning I wake at dawn, my anger dissipated, and make my way to the deck. Around me the sea heaves itself into blue-black peaks and furrows, marbled with foam. The sky is a soft grey, the wind sighs. At the westward end of the platform Nobby and Ginge are having a smoke, roll-ups cupped in their hands.

I've grown cautiously fond of our desolate outpost. Its physical boundaries are hard and unambiguous. For as long as we're here, we're alive. In the unlikely event that we stay that way, do Oxana and I have a future together?

Most relationships with psychopaths come to an end when the psychopath knows that their latest victim has succumbed, and so is no longer of interest. That's not how it is with us. We play with the notion of Oxana as the predator and me as her prey, but that's a game, and both of us know it. Right from the start, when she first looked into my eyes as Villanelle, Oxana recognised something that it would take time for me to understand. That we were fundamentally the same, and that in consequence neither of us could ever fully possess or control the other.

I think that this is why she acts up so obnoxiously, demanding my attention at the same time as rejecting it. She knows that I love her, but she also knows that the usual psychopathic love narrative, the one ending in my obliteration and her savage triumph, will not play out. Instead, it seems, we're moving towards a tentative equilibrium. I know that there's a place where I can't follow her. Where she has always been alone, and always will be. I tell myself that I can live with that. That all I have to do is be patient. Be waiting there with open arms when she returns.

This fragile optimism endures precisely until the moment when I walk into the canteen and see Charlie and Oxana sitting there, side by side. They have the sated, sleepy-eyed smugness of people who've been fucking all night. Charlie's fingers are splayed nonchalantly across Oxana's upper thigh, and Oxana's head is tilted proprietorially towards Charlie's.

The whole thing is so flagrant, so bare-faced and unapologetic, that for a moment I just stand there. How have I never noticed Charlie's fingers? Meaty, pink and spatulate, like the artisanal pork chipolatas Niko used to buy, and probably still does, from the West Hampstead farmers' market.

'Tea, *detka*?' Charlie asks Oxana, fixing me with eyes the colour of wet slate, and I feel my guts churn and my fists bunch uselessly at my side. I want, so badly, to hit them. No, let me amend that. Looking at those big chipolata fingers, and thinking of where they've been, I want to kill them. I want to kill them both.

Oxana shakes her head. She's got her blasé, what's-the-big-deal face on, and watches unblinking as I approach. 'Eve,' she says. 'Hi.'

'Fuck you,' I tell her, trying to keep my voice steady. 'Fuck you both.'

'Perhaps chill?' Charlie suggests, and without even thinking about it I reach for the nearest hard object, which turns out to be an unopened can of baked beans, and hurl it straight at them. The can catches Charlie right between the eyes. They collapse sideways off their chair, slide to the floor, and stay there.

Oxana stares at me speechlessly, her grey eyes wide. 'We're finished,' I tell her, picking up the dented can, slipping a finger through the ring-pull, and shaking the beans into a saucepan. 'Don't speak to me. And I hope the two of you are as happy together as pigs in shit.'

Anton walks in, and seeing Charlie slumped on the floor, stops dead. 'What the fuck's going on?' he asks, incredulous. 'You been fighting?'

I bang the saucepan down onto the Calor stove, and light the gas. 'You know how emotional we women get.'

On the floor Charlie stirs and groans. There's a lump the size of a walnut in the centre of their forehead, and a nasty-looking cut. A trail of blood runs into one eyebrow.

Anton looks at them irritably. 'So what happened to her?'

'Hit their head. They'll be fine.'

'Better be. You're her spotter. Find the first-aid box and get a dressing on that wound.'

'You fucking find it. I want my breakfast, and to be honest I don't care if Charlie lives or dies.'

Anton sneers. 'We're very full of piss and wind all of a sudden, aren't we? What brought that on? Girlfriend decide to start grazing in pastures new?'

I ignore him, and when Oxana stands Charlie's chair up, helps them to their feet, and examines the bump, I ignore her too. When the baked beans are ready I take the hot pan and a spoon outside to the deck, where I run into Nobby and Ginge.

'Lovely morning for it,' says Ginge, as he says every morning.

'Sure is,' I say. I've never eaten an entire tin of beans before.

When Charlie and I meet at the firing point, they've got a bandage around their head and regard me warily. Ginge clearly knows we've had a fight, but tactfully makes no reference to it. Instead, as I make the range and trace calls, my voice emptied of expression, Charlie puts round after round through the sniper rifle. Visibility is good, the sea is calm, and there's almost no crosswind. I can't have done Charlie any serious damage because we're soon knocking out the balloon targets at ranges of close to a kilometre.

'I wish there was more wind,' Charlie mutters to Ginge.

'Too easy, is it?'

'No, Eve keeps farting.'

'Ah.' He leans round and grins at me. 'I had a dog with that trouble. Good dog, mind.'

Somehow, the day passes. I hold on to my anger, keeping it icy and sharp inside me, and address not one word to Charlie that I don't have to. The sight of their bandage and the livid swelling beneath it consoles me a little. It was a brilliant reflex shot, though I say it myself, and I'm confident that they're not planning any immediate revenge.

They don't need to. Their triumph is complete. Why was I not prepared for Oxana to behave so viciously, so unforgivably, when in retrospect it was the most likely thing in the world? I know that she can't resist subjecting my feelings for her to cruel and wounding tests, and it was always probable that sooner or later she'd test them to destruction.

Fuck her. Seriously. I'm better off alone.

At the end of the day, a hard wind gets up and thin spits of snow come whirling in from the east. Standing on the edge of the platform in my combat clothes, my face pricking with the cold, I feel myself consumed by guilt and sadness. I gaze at the sea for what seems like a very long time, and as the light fades, and the feeling drains from my exposed face and hands, something in the vast indifference of the scene – some sad, steely note – possesses me, and my anger becomes determination. I may be empty inside, hollowed and devoured by Oxana, and I may be alone and beyond redemption, but I will not be broken.

Fuck them all.

I will not be broken.

# 9

The next day passes swiftly. I speak only when spoken to, ignore Oxana completely, and limit my exchanges with Charlie to calling the shots for them.

We have two nights left on the North Sea platform, then we return to Russia. At least I'm assuming that that's the case, as my passport contains no visa for any other country. Over the course of the day, I run through possible ways of contacting Tikhomirov. My only chance to do this will be when we've landed in Russia, and are making our way through the border controls. It will be impossible beforehand, while we are under the eye of Anton, and almost certainly impossible afterwards.

I consider different scenarios. A diversion of some kind, in the course of which I throw myself on the mercy of customs or security officials. A medical emergency, perhaps, with me writhing on the arrivals' hall floor with simulated gastroenteritis. Could I carry that off? Unlikely. Anton will be looking out for any hint of weird or erratic behaviour. He will keep us on a very short leash, and he's undoubtedly practised in dealing with the kind of functionaries you find at Russian airports.

Maybe I could try to steal a phone? The passport queue would be a possible place to lift one from a fellow traveller's back pocket or bag. All I would have to do would be to input Tikhomirov's number and let it ring. He would know it was me and be able to identify my location and track the phone. The penalty if I was discovered, however, would be severe, and given how closely we would all be watched, discovery was the probable outcome.

We've been working our way through our evening meal for the best part of fifteen minutes when I realise what's happening right in front of my eyes. Anton's watching us from the head of the table, and making entries in a small spiral notebook.

He's writing. With a pencil.

When he's finished Anton shoves the notebook in his trouser pocket and tosses the pencil onto a worktop, between a box of plastic spoons and a glass jar filled with teabags. Looking up, he catches my eye, and we exchange tight, non-committal smiles. Neither of us has quite worked out how we should conduct ourselves with each other. He's tried to have me killed at least twice, and I've never disguised the fact that I find him repulsive. It's not the ideal basis for a relationship.

I glance at the pencil. It's almost hidden behind the cardboard spoon-box, and as I look away a plan comes to me fully formed. It's dangerous, so dangerous that I can't bring myself to think of it in too much detail, but it's all I have. And weirdly, it brings me a sort of peace.

Sliding out of my bunk in combat clothes and socks, I open the door inch by inch, terrified that a squeak of hinges will betray me. Outside the cabin it's dark, but I've learnt the layout. I'm on a small landing, inside one of the platform's cylindrical legs. Bolted to the wall opposite me is a ladder, which runs upwards to the deck and downwards to the level of the sea. Below me is Ginge's cabin. Above me is Anton's. I've got to get past his door without him hearing me if I'm to get to the deck.

Taking a deep breath, I begin to climb the ladder. My socks are slippery on the cold steel rungs, and I can feel my heart pounding fearfully in my chest, but I force myself to keep going. There's no sound from Anton's cabin. I move upwards, and now I can hear the faint hum of the generator that provides the platform with power; it's housed in a hut next to the canteen.

As I haul myself through the hatch onto the platform deck, a gale-force wind whips my hair into my eyes. Above me the sky is a streaky blue-black, around me the sea is a roiling grey, faintly illuminated by the warning lights at each corner of the platform. I crouch there for a moment. I can no longer hear the generator, only the scream of the wind and the crashing of the waves. Then, keeping low, I run to the canteen and close the door behind me. Inside it's quieter, but no less cold. A couple of steps take me to the worktop, and I reach around the box of spoons for the pencil.

A moment later it's in my hand, and just as I feel its hexagonal shape between my fingers the door swings open and a torch shines in my face. The shock is so great that I stop breathing, and stare open-mouthed into the light.

'You deceitful cunt,' Anton says. 'I knew I was right about you.'

I can't see his face behind the torch beam, but I can imagine the sneer. There's no way I can escape. He's standing between me and the door.

'You were going to try and get a message out, weren't you? You saw me writing notes with a pencil and you thought, I'll have that. Well you know what, you dumb dyke, that's exactly what you were supposed to think. I left the pencil there knowing you'd come looking for it. You fucking women, honestly.'

Waves of fury wash through me. I feel weirdly focused and light-headed.

'I wish I'd saved everyone's time and killed you in St Petersburg. You and your psycho girlfriend. But hey, better late than never.' He reaches out with his free hand and grabs my arm, wrenching me towards the open door. I resist, pulling back hard, and as I do so I have the surreal impression that my body has been occupied by someone else. Someone strong, and ruthlessly efficient. Someone like Oxana.

I continue to pull away from Anton with all my strength, grunting with the effort, and then I jump forward, unbalancing him so that he falls heavily backwards and cracks his head on the steel door jamb. As he lies there, half-stunned and blinking in the raking torch beam, I shove the pencil as hard as I can up his left nostril.

Anton's eyes widen, his fingers writhe, and a quavering sound issues from his throat. He tries to lift his head, but I keep hold of the protruding end of the pencil and push downwards, forcing it further and further up his nose. The pencil sticks fast after about ten centimetres, so I put my weight behind it, and it slips in another couple of centimetres. Taking the torch from Anton's hand, I shine it in his face. His eyes have rolled back into his head, his lips are fluttering, and a worm of blood is crawling from his open nostril into his mouth.

'Fucking women,' I murmur. 'What can you do, eh?' The point of the pencil has almost certainly penetrated Anton's brain, but not lethally. I need something hard and heavy. 'Stay there,' I order him, and shine the torch around the canteen. Lying on the bookshelf is a substantial hardback volume. I'm reaching for this, when Anton half-rises to his feet, his eyes staring wildly. Grabbing the book with both hands I draw it back, take aim, and smack the pencil in another inch. He sinks to the floor, his legs moving feebly.

'Eve, sweetie, what's going on?'

I drop the book with a shriek, and clutch my heart. 'Jesus, Oxana.'

'What are you doing?'

'What the fuck does it look like I'm doing? Hammering a pencil into Anton's brain with a copy of *Birds of the North Sea*.'

'Is that good?'

'Definitive, according to the *Observer*.'

'No, that you're killing Anton. Was he annoying you?'

'He caught me stealing the pencil.'

'I don't understand.'

'It'll wait. Just hold his legs while I give it one last bash.'

When Anton finally stops shuddering I subside to an exhausted crouch against the container wall.

'Is he dead?' Oxana asks, flicking the end of the pencil with her finger.

163

'Near enough.'

She hunkers down opposite me, reaches for the torch, and switches it off. 'Night vision,' she explains.

I can't see much, but I can feel the warm bulk of Anton's body against my feet.

Oxana gives a long, phlegmy sniff. 'You really are quite the player, aren't you, *pupsik*?'

'Tell me why you're here.'

'I was looking for you. I went to your cabin and you weren't there.'

'Why were you looking for me?'

'I missed you.'

'Tough shit. Go and bunk up with Charlie.'

'Charlie's not you.'

'So why did you fuck them?'

'Well, technically speaking I didn't. We—'

'I don't want to know what you did, I just want to know why you did it.'

'I don't know. I just . . .' She sniffs again. 'Truthfully?'

'Truthfully.'

'Because I was angry with you.'

'Why?'

'Because I love you.'

'God, Oxana. Please.'

'I do. Truly.'

'In that case help me, because I need to get rid of this body? Over the edge of the platform.'

'OK, *pupsik*. Shall we take a leg each?'

'Don't call me that. I haven't forgiven you.'

'It was just a sex thing.'

'Sex things with other people are not OK, Oxana.'

164

'Sor-*ree* . . .' She glances at Anton. 'And you can stop looking at me like that, Pinocchio.'

It takes us several minutes to drag Anton out of the canteen to the westward end of the platform.

'Do you still want that pencil?' Oxana shouts, as the wind screams in our ears.

I've forgotten that securing the pencil was the point of the whole exercise. I nod and, kneeling beside Anton, try to pull it out of his nose with my fingertips. Anton's eyes roll in his head but I can't budge it, it's stuck tight.

Oxana tries, but does no better. She looks at me. 'The only way we're going to do this is if I hold his head, and you take the end of the pencil between your teeth and pull it out.'

'That's a really disgusting idea.'

'You're the one that wants the pencil, babe.'

'Yeah, I know. Fuck.'

'So do it.'

We do it. Oxana locks her fingers under Anton's jaw, and I lean sideways into his face and close my teeth on the end of the pencil. His lips are dry, his stubble rasps against my cheek, and his breath, now coming in shallow gasps, smells of brandy and curry. I pull at the pencil as hard as I can, but it doesn't move, and I'm afraid of snapping the end off with my teeth. Eventually I lift my head, gagging, and drag sea air into my lungs.

'Again,' Oxana mouths.

'You want a try?' I shout at her, and she shakes her head.

I take the pencil in my teeth again, brace my hands against Oxana's biceps, and pull as hard as I can. This time I feel something yielding. The pencil moves a millimetre or two, and as it finally slides out I feel liquid warmth bathe my neck and chest.

'Fuck,' I say. 'Blood everywhere.'

'Don't worry, sweetie, we'll deal with it. Sit back to back with me so I can kick this asshole over the edge.'

I feel her shoulders tense as she shoves with her legs, and when I look round Anton is gone. I don't even hear the splash.

We spend the next ten minutes tidying up. While I wash off the worst of the blood with water from the canteen, Oxana creeps into Anton's room and finds me a clean T-shirt and combat shirt. I pull these on, then we locate the Napoleon bottle, which is still half full, and take it outside. Oxana pours the remaining brandy over the edge of the platform, and leaves the empty bottle standing on deck. I knot my bloody clothes into a bundle and, using the torch as a sinker, throw them out to sea. Then, with the night's work completed, we depart the deck. Behind me, Oxana closes the hatch.

'Your cabin's in the south leg,' I tell her, but she takes no notice. Silently, rung by rung, she follows me down the steel ladder, past Anton's empty cabin, to mine. I turn on the light, we stand there for a moment, and then I pull back my arm and punch her in the mouth, as hard as I can. She flinches, blinks a couple of times, spits blood and snot into her hand, and wipes it down the thigh of her combat trousers.

'So,' she murmurs, licking her lips. 'Are we even now?'

I shake my head, wanting to hit her again, but discover that I'm shaking so much that I can't. I try to speak, but I can't do that either, because she's pulled my face down into the warm place between her shoulder and the slope of her breast, and has locked me there so tightly, with her cheek sealed against my forehead and her hand in my hair, that I can hardly breathe.

'Are we?' she asks, sniffing loudly in my ear, and all I can do is nod. She holds me for a time, and then lifts my face opposite hers.

'It didn't mean anything,' she says. 'It was just sex.'

'It was a shitty thing to do. Really nasty.'

'I know.'

'Do you have a tissue?'

'No. Do you need one?'

'No, but you do. That sniffing and swallowing thing you do is really gross.'

'I've got a cold, Eve. It happens. Even to Russians.'

'So do something about it. Jesus.'

She reaches into her pocket, pulls out a crumpled pair of knickers, and blows her nose into them. 'OK. Done.'

'And just for the record, have you had a shower since fucking Charlie?'

'Like I said, I didn't actually—'

'Have you?

'No.'

'Then have one now.'

'Eve, it's fuck-knows-what in the morning. I'll wake Ginge up.'

'I'm sure we won't. And it doesn't matter if we do, anyway, now that Anton's gone?'

'We?'

'I'm joining you. I feel disgusting.'

She narrows her grey cat's-eyes at me.

'Just don't speak, OK?'

She draws an imaginary zip across her mouth, but her lips are twitching.

We allow ourselves two luxurious minutes under the hot water. The first to wash off everything that's happened, the second to begin rediscovering each other. The tiny wash-room is not the ideal space for a date, but it's warm and steamy, and Oxana is strong. Strong enough to lift me up the wall until her face is between my thighs and my legs are over her shoulders and I'm leaning back, open-mouthed and gasping, against the wet tiles.

In my narrow bunk, with her body warm against mine and the smell of her in my nostrils, we huddle under the thin blankets and swap recollections of our first encounters.

'It was that hot, thundery evening in Shanghai,' she whispers. 'We just saw each other for a second in the street, but it was electric. It was like looking at myself. That's why I climbed into your room at the hotel and watched you sleep. To make sure it was true.'

'And was it? Is it?'

'You know the answer to that. You proved it tonight. Are you going to tell me why you wanted that pencil so much?'

'I'll tell you tomorrow. I don't want to think about all that. I want us to be here, in this bunk, in this cabin, for ever.'

'I know, *pchelka*, me too. One day.'

'One day.'

'*Spoki noki*, baby bee.'

'Sweet dreams.'

\*

When Anton doesn't show up for breakfast the next morning, no one takes much notice. The empty brandy bottle at the edge of the platform has been noted, and Nobby and Ginge make sympathetic references to hangovers and mornings after. By eight-thirty, however, the two men are looking at their watches and exchanging concerned glances. Ginge offers to go to Anton's cabin and wake him, and when he returns he looks grave.

He and Nobby confer, then we split up and search every inch of the platform. It doesn't take long. The two office containers are locked, but a glance through the windows tells us they're unoccupied.

'There wasn't any kind of boat or inflatable craft he could have taken?' I suggest helpfully, and Ginge shakes his head.

'No. And even if there was, it was blowing at least force eight last night. The boss wouldn't have been crazy enough to try anything like that.'

'Only possible conclusion, he went over the side,' Nobby says. 'Probably after downing that bottle.'

'Deliberately?' I ask.

'Nah. Why would he? He was well up for this project and obviously wanted to see it through. Probably got pissed up and lost his footing. Easily done.'

Ginge nods. 'Question is, what do the rest of us do now? We've got twenty-four hours until the chopper comes to pick us up.'

'Carry on as before?' Oxana suggests. 'It doesn't need to make any difference.'

'I can be your spotter today,' Nobby says.

'Sure. Whatever.'

Ginge looks from face to face. 'Everyone OK with that? We carry on as we were? Meanwhile I'll see what I can do about the lock on that front office. Pretty sure there's a satphone in there and that the antenna works.'

'Who you gonna call?' Nobby asks. 'Ghostbusters?'

'Our employers. Give them a heads-up about the boss.'

'Rather you than me.'

'Got to be done, boyo.'

We return to the firing points. The sea and the sky are calmer today, and visibility much improved. Charlie's nailing pretty much every target at seven hundred metres plus, now. One shot, one kill, as Ginge continually impresses on us. From what I can see, Oxana's hit rate is every bit as consistent.

We spend our last night on the platform in my cabin. I tell Oxana about the encounter with Tikhomirov, and how he asked me to contact him if I discover what the Twelve are planning, and I say that, if possible, I intend to do exactly this. The more important our target is, I argue, the less likely it is that the Twelve will let us walk away when the job's done. We're more than expendable, we're a liability.

If I can make contact with Tikhomirov, on the other hand, and provide him with enough information to intercept us before we fire a shot, he may see an advantage in keeping us alive, and letting it be known that we were acting as his agents all along. Oxana is briefly angry that I didn't tell her earlier and deeply suspicious of any alliance with the FSB, but agrees that in the long run we are probably marginally better off relying on the state security service than the Twelve.

'And this is what you wanted the pencil for?' she asks me.

'Exactly. To try to get a message to him.'

I tell her my plan, such as it is, and she considers it in silence.

'Could work,' she says eventually, stroking my cheek with cold-roughened fingers. 'At the same time I'd kind of like to go through with the hit. I'd love to pull the trigger on someone really high profile. Just to sign off.'

'I wish you didn't enjoy it so much.'

'I'm good at it. Every ocean needs its sharks. Every kill I've carried out has left the world a better place.'

'That's not what it's about, though, is it? I mean, you're not really interested in making the world a better place.'

'Mmm . . . no. Maybe not.'

'And you're not a sadist. You don't get turned on watching people suffer.'

'Not particularly.' She slides her hand down my back. 'Apart from you, obviously.'

'Very funny. And stop wobbling my bum.'

'I love your bum.'

'Easy for you to say, with a body like a weasel on steroids. But go on. Remind me. What is it about murder that turns you on so much?'

'I could ask you the same question.'

'Meaning?'

'Meaning not to be that bitch, sweetie, but you're a murderer too. Twice over.'

'Well, yeah, OK, but both of those were . . .'

'Were?'

'You know perfectly well. I had no choice.'

'And I did? You really think I could say no, sorry, Konstantin, I can't carry out your contract. I've got a hair-dressing appointment at Carita in the morning, then lunch at Arpège, and in the afternoon I was planning to hack into Eve Polastri's email, masturbate, and eat a box of Fauchon marrons glacés.'

'You did that?'

'What, eat a whole box of marrons glacés at one go?'

'Hack into my email and masturbate?'

'I tried. But it wasn't interesting. No sexy messages. No nude selfies.'

'Why would I take nude selfies?'

'For me to find, obviously. I wasn't going to finger myself over your bank statements. But back to you, *pupsik*. You're so many things. You're an ex-spy, although if we're being honest not a great one. You're Niko the asshole's ex-wife. You're my current lover.'

'Current?'

'Yes. Means right now.'

'I know what it means. I speak English. It's just a bit . . . Couldn't you just say you're my lover?'

She nips my cheek with her teeth. 'I'm teasing you. But yeah. You're clever, a bit nerdy, and quite needy. You're a scaredy-cat but also weirdly brave. You're sexy and adorable in bed and you're a really, really terrible cook.'

'How do you know?'

'I've seen inside your fridge. It was tragic.'

'Anything else?'

'Yes, you have zero fashion sense.'

'Thanks.'

'The point I'm making is this. That if I took all these things away from you, if I peeled it all away, layer by layer, there'd still be you. Underneath everything, there's Eve. And you know that about yourself, you know exactly who you are. But I don't have that. If I take away everything I've done, and all the people I've been, or pretended to be – all the layers – there's nothing. No Villanelle, no Oxana, no self at all, just a . . .' She's silent for a moment. 'Did you see that film, *The Invisible Man*? You couldn't see him, but you could see the effect he had on the things and the people around him. That's how I feel. The only reason I know that there's a me, an Oxana, is that I see the trail she leaves. I see the fear and the horror in people's eyes, and that tells me that she exists – that I exist. Konstantin understood this perfectly. He knew that I needed to make the world echo with my presence.'

'And this made you feel powerful?'

'It made me feel alive. Those kills that I carried out for Konstantin were beautiful. Perfectly planned, perfectly executed. Fucking works of art, to be honest.'

'And you want one more hit of that drug before you walk away? One more smack rush? One last high?'

'Maybe I do.'

'But can't you see? If that's what it takes to make you feel alive, you'll never walk away. There'll be one more kill, and then one more, and one more after that. Until someone kills you.'

'I'll walk away, trust me.'

'Why would you?'

'Because killing for the Twelve is not the only thing that makes me feel alive. Not any more.'

'What else does?'

'You, *pupsik*. You do. You look at me with such tenderness, and such love. For the first time since I was a child, since that visit to the Kungur ice caves, I feel seen. I feel that there's someone there, underneath all the bullshit. A real Oxana. A real me.'

'But my loving you is obviously not enough, since you still want one last kill.'

She shrugs. 'If it's some real high-end evil motherfucker I wouldn't want the job to go to anyone else.'

'Supposing it's someone not evil at all? Supposing it's a woman?'

'I've never killed a woman.'

'That's very sisterly of you.'

'I didn't say I wouldn't, I just said I hadn't.'

'Truth is, we don't have any choice about any of this. When the time comes they're going to deliver us to our firing points, and we're just going to have to do it or get killed. If I try to get a word to Tikhomirov, at least we've got a chance.'

'What would you tell him? We don't know anything useful. No who, no where, no when, no why.'

'You're right, we don't. All we know is the range. And that's not much help.'

'Do you think Nobby and Ginge know the target?'

'They don't need to, so no, I don't. They're just old army mates of Anton's. And I doubt he knew, either.'

'It'll be very soon.'

'Why do you say that?'

'Because I know how the Twelve work. Everything's arranged so you're not left hanging around. You're given time to prepare, but not too much time, because the longer you keep people waiting, the more likely it is that there'll be some kind of security issue. My guess is that it'll be within a couple of days of our leaving here.'

'We don't have much time then.'

'No, *pupsik*, we don't. So stop talking and come here.'

# IO

The helicopter comes for us at midday. Aboard are two Twelve paramilitaries, both carrying sidearms. They jump down onto the platform, carry out a thorough search of the entire installation, nod cursorily at Nobby and Ginge, and shepherd us on board the Super Puma. As we swing away into the wind I peer downwards, suddenly fearful that Anton's body will appear, arms outstretched, borne up by the choppy waves. But there's nothing, no accusing corpse, only the diminishing figures of Nobby and Ginge on the platform, and the grey wastes of the sea.

At Ostend, the two men keep us on a short rein, fast-tracking us through security and passport control and marching us out onto the tarmac, where the Learjet is fuelled up and waiting. I squeeze Oxana's hand as we take off, and keep hold of it. Our destination, as expected, is Moscow. The engine noise is little more than a discreet hum, but I'm too nervous to talk.

When faced by danger, Oxana and I are polar opposites. I foresee terrible outcomes, and become possessed by fear, while Oxana's sense of impending threat is so shallow as to barely register. As her body prepares itself for action, her mind remains calm. It must be the same for Charlie, who lounges back in their seat, chewing gum that they've some-how extracted from the soldiers, and studiously ignores us.

'Are you all right?' Oxana asks.

I nod. There's so much to say, and I can't say any of it.

'Glad you left England with me?'

I touch her cheek. 'Did I have a choice?'

'I know what's best for you, *pchelka*. Just trust me, OK. I know there was the Charlie thing, but seriously. Trust me.'

'I'm worried now. What do you know that I don't?'

'Nothing. I'm just saying. Whichever way this thing plays out.'

'Shit, sweetie. Talk to me.'

'I don't know anything, I'm just saying. Trust me. Trust us.'

'I'm so scared.'

'I know, babe.'

Scared or not, I proceed with my plan. After breakfast on the platform I surreptitiously tore a small blank strip from a page of *Birds of the North Sea* and glued it into the back of my passport, using a couple of dabs of honey. Now, as soon as we're airborne, I take out my hard-won pencil and write, heading the message with the telephone number that I've memorised, and asking the person reading it to call the number urgently, on a matter of state security, and deliver the following message to General Tikhomirov: *2 shooters, this week, range 700m.*

Shortly before we begin our descent to Moscow, one of the paramilitaries collects our passports, securing them with an elastic band. We seem to circle the city for ever, and as we go through landing and disembarkation procedures at Sheremetyevo I'm so terrified I almost vomit. If the para-military examines the passports, as he well may, that'll be the end. If I'm lucky, it'll be a bullet in the back of the head. I don't want to think of the alternatives.

Entering the airport buildings, we're fast-tracked through a small VIP customs hall. There are two officers, dressed in bulky green winter uniforms. An older woman with tiny, granite eyes, and a shaven-headed young man whose broad-brimmed cap is several sizes too large for him.

Our paramilitary chaperone takes our passports from his pocket, removes the elastic band, and as he flicks through the pages of the top passport before passing it to the woman, I feel my knees begin to shake. I'm guessing that my face has gone white, because Oxana puts an arm round me and asks if I'm all right. I nod, and the other Twelve guy peers at me suspiciously. 'Delayed reaction,' I stammer. 'Flying. I get very nervous.'

'Give them all to me,' the granite-eyed woman orders. Her name-tag identifies her as Lapotnikova, Inna. Taking the passports, she opens the first, looks up, and beckons Charlie to the counter. I'm second in line after Charlie. I watch Ms Lapotnikova slowly page through the forgery, and come to a halt as she reaches the page with the note. She reads it expressionlessly, and slowly looks up at me, one eyebrow raised questioningly. I nod imperceptibly and she discreetly pulls out the note and returns my passport to me. Then handing the remaining three passports to her colleague, she unhurriedly leaves the room.

For a moment I'm weak with relief, then it occurs to me that she may simply have gone to call airport security. Perhaps she thinks I'm some deranged conspiracy theorist.

Either way, I'm finished. Under my suddenly too-hot clothes I feel a sweat-bead running down my spine. I try to look casual and Oxana squeezes my hand. 'Relax,' she murmurs. 'You look like you're trying not to shit.'

Lapotnikova returns just as the customs officer in the big hat is handing back the last of the passports. She ignores me and returns to her seat. I want to hug her. We're through. I've done everything I can, the rest is up to Tikhomirov, although whether my message will be the slightest help to him, I don't know. I'm guessing not.

We're driven back to Moscow in the same SUV, this time by one of our armed guards. The second guy sits in the passenger seat with his pistol in his lap, presumably in case one of us tries to filch it from its holster. I'm in the back seat, as usual, between Oxana and Charlie. The symbolism of this arrangement is not lost on Charlie, who stares pointedly out of the window for the entire journey. Oxana, kittenish at the prospect of action, creeps her fingers under my sweater and round my waist, tickling and pinching me.

'Do you know the expression "muffin top"?' she whispers.

As we approach central Moscow, we're forced to negotiate street barriers, road closures and diversions. 'What's going on?' I ask the driver, as the traffic slows to a standstill.

'New Year's Eve celebrations,' he answers, irritably negotiating a three-point turn.

'Not tonight, surely?' I've lost all track of the date.

'No. Day after tomorrow.'

*

We're delivered back to the twelfth floor of the grey skyscraper and shown to our old rooms. I'm scared, in a generalised sort of way, but mostly I'm just very, very hungry. Whatever tomorrow holds, there's tonight's dinner to look forward to, followed by a night in a full-sized bed with Oxana. For now, that's enough.

Below us, as dusk falls, Moscow lights up. The New Year decorations are in place, and the streets, cathedrals and skyscrapers are a blaze of gold and silver and sapphire. Gazing out of the window, I think how wonderful it would be to be able to explore the city with Oxana, unburdened with fear and horror and dreams of death, and lose ourselves in the dazzle and enchantment of it all.

At dinner, Richard questions us closely about Anton. Charlie does most of the talking, explaining that the general consensus was that he'd been drinking late at night, and had fallen off the platform.

'You knew him better than anyone else, Villanelle. How did he strike you?'

'He was like he always was. I never liked him that much but he was professional, and ran things properly. Everything was well organised, supplies, weaponry, all that. And then one morning he just wasn't there.'

'Eve?'

'What can I say? I couldn't stand the man, but like Oxana says everything ran smoothly. I just kept out of his way.'

'Lara?'

'My name's Charlie. And yeah. What the others said. But I'm pretty sure he was drinking. I was making myself coffee one morning before breakfast, and he came in smelling of alcohol, like it was coming out of his skin. Obviously I didn't say anything to him, but—'

'Did you tell either of the instructors?'

'They didn't ask me. And after he disappeared I didn't want to say negative things about him in case people blamed me. But it's true.'

I glance at Charlie. They're looking at me, not with hatred or jealousy, but levelly, as if to say that now we're square, and I give them the ghost of a nod.

Richard brightens. 'Who'd like some wine? It's the Château Pétrus.'

'What, again?' Oxana says.

He smiles. 'We must celebrate your return. Seasonal greetings, and all that. I believe our little North Sea getaway is quite chilly at this time of year.' He fills our glasses. 'Good luck to you, ladies.'

'And to me,' says Charlie.


The next day passes with stifling slowness. We're not permitted to leave the twelfth floor, or to do anything except pace around like zoo animals, breathing the building's recycled air. There are no books, no newspapers, no computers or phones. Oxana and I have temporarily run out of things to say to each other, and I spend most of the afternoon sleeping. After dinner Richard announces a film show, and we follow him into a projection room with a screen covering most of one wall. 'It's not long, and there's no sound,' he tells us, as we take our places. 'But it's quite an eye-opener.'

There are no titles, just a recording date and a time code. Then a silent, wide-angle shot of a hotel suite from a fixed camera, almost certainly concealed. The quality of the film isn't great, but this is clearly a very upscale, thousands-of-dollars-a-night sort of place. The colour scheme is parchment and oak, the curtains are ivory silk, the lighting is discreet. Two men in suits, holding whisky tumblers, sit in armchairs on either side of a marble fireplace. Both are immediately recognisable. One is Valery Stechkin, the president of Russia, the other is Ronald Loy, president of the United States. Both have the rouged, powdered look of the recently embalmed. A third man, with the watchful demeanour of a bodyguard, stands by a door.

'Not lookalikes?' I ask Richard.

'Absolutely not.'

Stechkin and Loy stand, place their empty tumblers on the mantelpiece, and shake hands. Loy then walks Stechkin to the door. The film cuts and then reprises from the same viewpoint with lower lighting as the door opens and three young women walk in. They're all blonde, long-legged, and spectacular in a listless, stoned sort of way. Loy leans back in his chair, nods, and issues an order. The women undress, drape their clothes over the vacant armchair, and start kissing and caressing each others' breasts with much eye-rolling and simulated groaning.

'Get on with it,' Oxana mutters.

Eventually we're treated to the full three-way performance. It's pretty dispiriting. Loy doesn't join in, but sits back in his chair, his expression disdainful. When one of the women experimentally waggles a glistening strap-on in front of his nose, he responds irritably, batting it away with a tiny, childlike hand.

The film cuts to a bedroom furnished in the same rich, fustian colours. The bed itself is enormous and covered in

183

gold damask. The three women walk into the shot, followed by Loy. He orders them to climb onto the bed, where they bounce up and down in a desultory fashion before coming to a halt, crouching down, and as one, beginning to urinate onto the gold coverlet.

From his chair, Loy stares at the women through narrowed eyes, as if watching them was a wearisome but essential presidential duty. Halfway through the process, one of the women overbalances on her high heels and tips forward, sliding off the bed in a torrent of piss.

'It's all in her hair,' says Charlie. 'Yuck.'

'And those suede boots are ruined,' adds Oxana.

'They're really nice. Or they were.'

'They're Prada. In Paris, I had two pairs. One in camel and one in anthracite.'

'That girl on the left's been peeing for almost a minute,' Charlie says. 'She should go on *Russia's Got Talent*.'

Finally, blessedly, the scene comes to a close.

'Oh boo,' Oxana protests. 'I was really enjoying that.'

The lights come up in the room, and Richard looks at us one by one. 'Villanelle, I'm happy that you liked the show but it wasn't intended as light entertainment. That short clip has had a greater impact on world history than any political event, debate, or policy decision in the last decade. Holding this trump card, this *kompromat*, has enabled Stechkin to steer the White House as he chooses. Not just to steer it but to throw it into a catastrophic reverse. Meanwhile the Russian Federation over which he presides like a latter-day Roman emperor is sclerotic and corrupt to the core.

'I'm telling you this because I want you to believe in what we, here, are trying to achieve. The new world we dream of will not be brought about by democratic process, that dream is dead. It'll be brought about by decisive action, and you three are going to be the prime movers of that action. Your targets are Ronald Loy and Valery Stechkin, the presidents of the United States and Russia. They die tomorrow.'

'And the girls?' Charlie asks.

'What girls?'

'The girls in the film.'

'What about them?'

'We don't have to kill them?'

'No, of course not.'

'Phew.'

'So when do we get a proper briefing?' Oxana asks. 'Tomorrow's cutting it very fine. We need to recce the firing points, prepare the weapons, all that.'

'Everything's checked and ready. You don't have to worry. You'll be taken to your locations, where you'll find everything you need, and last-minute details will be dealt with in situ. So get a good night's sleep.'

Unsurprisingly, I can't do any such thing. I lie with my back to Oxana, who has her arm around me and her face in my hair, trying to find a gleam of hope in what lies ahead.

'I know why I was chosen to be part of this,' I tell her. 'It's so that if everything goes wrong, they can point at me and say that the whole thing was cooked up by MI6. I'm their alibi.'

'Mmm. Also true that the only way they were going to get me – the best – was to take you too.'

'I just wish there was some way out.'

'There isn't, *pupsik*. But it's not as if you're going to be pulling the trigger.'

'I know that. I just want us to end up together. Not dead or imprisoned for life.'

'We're not dead yet.'

'Not yet.'

Her arm tightens and she presses herself against me. 'Trust me, *pchelka*.'

'I do. I love you.'

'I love you too. Now go to sleep.'

In the morning she's not there when I wake, and nor are her clothes. I pace the corridor, and look in all the rooms that aren't locked, but she's gone, and I feel wretched. At breakfast, there's just Charlie and me. We sit in silence. They wolf down a full cooked breakfast. I manage a bread roll with gooseberry jam and coffee.

Afterwards, no one comes for us, although there are the usual anonymous figures going in and out of the offices. So we sit in the restaurant area, staring out of the windows. It hasn't snowed since we arrived back in Moscow, and the sky is a cold, hard blue. On the building's exterior, icicles hang from the window ledges.

'We should get our cold-weather gear ready,' Charlie says. 'Thermals, gloves, hats, all that stuff. We might have to lie up for hours at the firing point.'

They're right. I assemble the warmest clothes I've been issued, and leave everything else in my room. I'm under no illusion that I'm ever going to see it again. Hours pass, lunch comes and goes. I feel a nauseated apprehension, but Charlie's appetite is unflagging.

Afterwards they fold their arms and look at me. 'You killed Anton, didn't you?'

'What the fuck, Charlie?'

'I knew him a lot better than you did, and he wasn't a drinker. He hated the idea of losing control.'

I shake my head. 'Sorry, but that's crazy. I mean seriously, why would I kill him? And more to the point, how?'

'I don't know how. But I'll tell you what's crazy. That story of him drinking half a bottle of brandy and falling off the edge of the platform? There's no way he'd let that happen.'

'Look, I don't know what happened to him, OK? End of story.'

Charlie smiles. 'I'm not going to say anything, Eve. But I just wanted you to know that I know. OK?'

'Whatever, Charlie.'

# II

They come for us in late afternoon, when the light is beginning to fail. There's Richard, incongruously dressed in a Russian army greatcoat, a hard-eyed young guy with a submachine gun slung over his leather jacket, and an older man in a crumpled coat carrying what looks like a miner's helmet.

Richard greets us, and introduces his companions as Tolya and Gennadi. 'All set?' he asks, and Charlie and I indicate that we are. Dry-mouthed with apprehension, I follow them all to the end of the corridor, where Richard inputs the door exit code, and summons the lift. We descend in silence to a basement, two floors below ground level, and step out into cold darkness. Richard touches a switch, illuminating a dusty, damp-smelling Aladdin's cave of packing cases, electrical generator components, construction materials, ladders, rusting fridges and travelling trunks, among which I can distinctly hear the scurrying of rats.

We follow Richard through this detritus to a steel door set into a central column. He tilts his head towards an overhead camera, waits for the facial-recognition software to execute, and pushes the heavy door open. Ahead of us an iron spiral staircase descends into darkness. A click, and a succession of fluorescent lamps flickers into life. Richard and Gennadi lead, Charlie and I follow, Tolya brings up the rear. There's an icy, sulphurous updraught which grows stronger the further we descend, and I'm glad of my thermals and cold-weather gear.

Finally we reach a concrete floor. Richard takes a torch from his pocket, and Gennadi puts on his helmet and switches on the headlight. We follow them into a dark tunnel, the lights illuminating weeping brick walls and an iron walkway. From beneath the walkway comes the sound of rushing water. It's rank-smelling and creepy as fuck.

'What is this place?' I whisper.

'People call it the reverse world,' Richard says. 'That water you can hear is the Neglinka river, diverted underground in the eighteenth century. There's a whole network of tunnels, sewers and watercourses down here. In the old days, there were also KGB listening posts. Gennadi used to work in one. He's one of the few remaining *kroty*, moles, who know their way around the network.'

'You could get lost down here and no one would ever find you,' Gennadi tells me, his headlight beam sweeping across a crop of greyish mushrooms growing from the brickwork. 'I've seen skeletons down here. Most of them from Stalin's time. You can tell by the holes in the back of the skulls.'

'Jesus.'

'Jesus never came down here,' Gennadi says grimly.

The brick tunnel comes to an abrupt end and we step out into a chamber supported by arches of discoloured brick and lit by strings of low-wattage electric bulbs. Iron walkways run the length of the chamber and bridge a deep channel through which river water is flowing. With a shock I see men and women moving in the dark shadows by the walls.

'Who are they?' I ask Gennadi and he shrugs.

'Addicts, ex-convicts, hermits . . . Some of them live down here for months at a time.'

There are about twenty of them in the group. Pale, ageless figures, dressed in threadbare uniforms and coats, who stare at us incuriously as we approach. One, a thin young woman with pinched features, points a finger at me accusingly, her mouth working in silent anger. I'm shaken to see people living in a place like this but Charlie seems unfazed. Perhaps if you've done time in a prison like Butyrka nothing ever seems weird again.

We follow the beam of Gennadi's headlamp along the narrow pathway beside the river channel. Shining stalactites hang from the vaulted brick ceiling. At intervals waterdrops fall from these to the river surface, the percussive sound echoing in the silence. We continue for ten minutes, perhaps more, and I become aware of a distant rushing sound. This gradually builds in volume until we reach a weir, where the river cascades over the lip of the channel into a pool some five metres below.

'OK, difficult bit,' Gennadi says. 'Tunnel is behind waterfall.'

'I'll go first,' Richard says. 'I've done this before.'

Handing Gennadi his torch, he begins to descend a steel ladder affixed to the vertical face of the ledge on which we're standing. At any other time, the sight of a senior MI6 officer in an overcoat and tie climbing into an underground river would be noteworthy, but I have seen so much that is terrifying and strange in recent days that I barely give it a thought. And then Richard appears to vanish.

I stare at Gennadi and he grins. 'You go next. You'll see.'

Nervously, I begin a torchlit descent of the cold, wet rungs. Beneath me, in the darkness, the river churns and roars. Then Gennadi angles the torch beam behind the waterfall, and I see that there's a gap just wide enough to slip through. Beyond it, just visible in the wavering beam, is the interior of yet another tunnel. Richard steps into view, and extends an arm. I take it, and as I half-step, half-leap towards the tunnel, he hauls me inside.

'Fuck,' I gasp.

'All right?' Richard asks.

'Just about.'

When the others have crossed safely, Richard turns to a door facing us a short distance up the tunnel. This is protected by a number code, which he taps in, masking the keypad with his body. As the door swings open, he and Gennadi shake hands. 'Go safely,' says the mole, raising a hand to us before stepping back behind the waterfall. Soon the beam from his helmet is no longer visible.

A pale light, however, shines from behind the half-open door. We're on a walkway near the top of a huge cylindrical shaft. Below us, staircases descend in a series of zigzags for at least a hundred metres. Richard loses no time, beckoning us to follow him. We descend the stairways at speed, passing floor after floor, our boots thudding on the metal treads. The deeper we go, the eerier the place looks. The steel-ribbed walls are coated with flaking red anti-rust paint, while the fittings look decades old. Scuffed dust and flattened cigarette ends suggest that others have used these stairs recently, and after a time a faint hum becomes audible from below. It takes us about ten minutes to reach the bottom of the stairs and a makeshift atrium where an armed guard waits for us, the winged shield on his uniform identifying him as an officer of GUSP, the former 15th Directorate of the KGB. The espionage nerd in me can't help being a tiny bit thrilled at this. In London, we knew GUSP as the most secretive of the Russian security services. We had no idea what they actually did.

Richard shows identification and the officer nods us past. An automatic door opens in front of us, the sulphurous smell is suddenly stronger, and we follow a corridor into a scene so unreal that Charlie and I both stop dead. We are on the deserted platform of an underground railway station. Both to the left and the right the track vanishes into unlit tunnels. Opposite us, on a wall faced with glazed tiles, is a bronze hammer and sickle a metre high and an enamel sign reading D6-EFREMOVA.

'What is this?' I ask Richard.

'Efremova station,' he answers. 'Part of the D-6 underground network. Officially, D-6 doesn't exist. Unofficially, it was built by Stalin to link the Kremlin to underground KGB command posts, and to evacuate the Politburo and the generals from Moscow in the event of nuclear war. Work on it has continued in secret ever since.'

'I've heard the rumours,' Charlie says, looking around them. 'Everyone has. But I thought it was just *dezinformatsiya.*'

Richard smiles. 'You know what they say. The greatest trick the Devil ever pulled was convincing the world he didn't exist. That's the KGB all over.'

'So what happens now?' I ask Tolya, who has yet to utter a single word.

In answer he nods towards Richard.

'It's very simple,' Richard says. 'We wait for our train.'

So we stand there, Richard dressed like a commuter bound for a day's work at a London investment bank, Charlie and I zipped into our black cold-weather gear like skiers at an Alpine resort, and Tolya looking like a Mafia enforcer.

'So if the D-6 network is a secret Russian government asset, how do you and the Twelve have access to it?'

Richard frowns thoughtfully. 'Eve, there are things I'm not at liberty to explain. Let's just say . . . It's complicated.'

He's saved from further explanation by the arrival of the train. It's a single carriage, clearly many decades old, with an electric locomotive at each end. We climb aboard. The interior is functional but worn, with a single flickering light, threadbare upholstery, and discoloured windows part-covered by curtains. We sit down, the doors close with a faint hydraulic hiss, and the train draws away from the platform into the darkness.

'Remember this journey,' Richard tells Charlie and me, as Tolya looks on silently. 'No one would believe you if you told them you'd ridden the deep rail. They'd think you were crazy, or a fantasist.'

Soon we pass through another station – I glimpse a sign reading D6-VOLKHONKA through the grimy glass – but the train doesn't stop until we reach D6-CENTRAL. The whole journey has taken less than ten minutes. Stepping from the train, regretfully in my case, we exit into an atrium very like the one at Efremova, except that this time there are half-a-dozen GUSP officers guarding the deserted station. In the place of Efremova's stairways, a succession of escalators rises within the steel-walled shaft. It takes several minutes to reach the top level, where we alight into a dusty, littered hallway with several exit corridors radiating from it.

Richard leads us to the furthermost of these, which is signposted NIKOLSKAYA. There's a light-switch on the concrete wall though he ignores it, preferring to follow the pale beam of his torch. I can feel a cold breeze and the beating of my heart.

The corridor goes in a dead straight line. There's smashed glass on the ground and puddles of dark water. At one point the torch beam catches a pair of shining eyes, and a cat bolts out of the shadows. Finally, we reach a dead end. There's an aluminium stepladder leaning against the wall, which Tolya stands up and climbs before pushing open a steel hatch over his head.

'This is where I say goodbye, good luck, and good hunting,' Richard tells us. 'Tolya, you know what to do.'

Tolya nods, and effortlessly pulls himself up into the darkness. Charlie follows. I climb the ladder, jam my elbows through the gap, and with Tolya's help manage to haul myself onto a cold stone floor, where I collapse for several seconds.

'You OK?' Charlie whispers, not unkindly.

'Yep. Thanks.'

Tolya gives us a couple of minutes to acquire our night vision. 'OK,' he says eventually, speaking for the first time. 'More climbing.'

We make our way upwards in near darkness. We're inside a tower, musty-smelling and ancient. A narrow stair ascends through three wooden floors, past high Gothic windows through which bright lights are visible, to a small, eight-faceted chamber. The windows are narrow and have not been cleaned in years, and several of the smaller panes are cracked or missing, admitting ice-cold air and the sound of singing and shouting.

I peer outside. Some sixty metres below us lies the glittering, illuminated expanse of Red Square, teeming with New Year revellers. On the far side of the square is the GUM department store, its towers and turrets strung with golden bulbs, and in front of the store, shimmering beneath a bank of spotlights, is an outdoor ice-rink, around which skaters are whirling, weaving and occasionally colliding as pop music booms from loudspeakers. In any other circumstances this festive scene would be intoxicating; tonight, it's terrifying. It's like my first glimpse of the stage on which I am to be performing a leading role, despite knowing none of my lines.

The D-6 underground railway, I realise, has enabled us to bypass multiple layers of security checks and CCTV surveillance, and insert ourselves, unseen, into the interior of the Kremlin itself. I calculate that we must be in one of the historic towers on the eastern wall. On the floor, in a hard-shell case, is the AX rifle, the Nightforce scope, and a suppressor. Beside it is a box of Lapua .338 Magnum rounds, a Leupold spotting scope in its case, two wireless headsets, a thermos flask, and a plastic sandwich box containing sandwiches, a chocolate bar and caffeine tablets.

As Charlie sets up the rifle, and I busy myself with the spotter scope, Tolya switches on one of the headsets, speaks briefly, and passes a set to each of us. There's ten seconds of

dead air, then a flat, disembodied voice requires us to identify ourselves as 'Charlie' and 'Echo'. We do so and are told
to prepare our equipment and report when ready. Tolya
then wishes us good luck, and takes the narrow stairway
downwards to the floor below to keep guard. The thermos
contains hot sugared coffee, and I pour myself a cup.

'Charlie ready.'

'Echo ready.'

'In your location, there are eight windows. With your
back to the entrance, note the window at eleven o'clock.
You will see that two of the lower panes have been removed.
You will direct your telescopic sights and spotter scope
through these.'

'Done.'

'Done.'

'Opposite you is a red-brick museum with white turrets
and roofs. From your position, draw an imaginary line to
the ridge of the highest roof. You have approximately one
metre clearance, minus the depth of the snow on the roof.
Tell me when you have done this.'

'Done.'

'Done.'

'Continue along that line for four hundred metres,
between the high buildings, and you will see ornamental
gardens on your right. Cross the highway and your line cuts
through the north-east corner of a square with a circular
fountain at its centre. The last hundred metres takes you to
the front of a building with eight pillars in front of three
double entrance doors. Do you see?'

'Yes, Echo seen.'

'Charlie seen.'

'Echo, give me your range to the central pillar.'

'Seven hundred and thirteen point five three.'

'Charlie, confirm.'

'Confirmed.'

'Echo, how is visibility?'

'Excellent.'

'Crosswind?'

'Negative.'

'Very well. The time now is nine minutes past six. At half past seven the car carrying the two targets will descend the one-way street running alongside the eastern side of the theatre. You will be given warning of its approach. It will halt by the eastern pillar, and the targets will exit the car and walk behind the pillars to either the first or the central doorway. Your target is the Russian. Repeat, your target is the Russian. There will be bodyguards and others with the group, so correct identification is paramount. You will have, at most, fifteen seconds in which to identify and dispatch your target. One shot, one kill. Heard?'

'Echo heard.'

'Charlie heard.'

'Good. Keep this channel open. Remain at the firing point. Remain silent and vigilant. Be aware that you are potentially visible from below.'

'You know what that building is?' Charlie asks. 'The one with the pillars?'

'A theatre?'

'*The* theatre. That's the Bolshoi.'

It gets colder, and colder still. We finish the coffee, and Charlie takes a caffeine tab. 'I'm glad we've got Stechkin.'

'Why?' I ask.

'Because he's shorter than Loy. They've given me the harder target.'

'So Oxana's got Loy?'

'Obviously.'

My elbows and knees gradually lose all feeling on the floor. 'I'm desperate to pee,' I say, after a time.

'So pee,' Charlie says.

'Where?'

'Anywhere. On the floor?'

'It'll go through the boards. Onto Tolya.'

'In the sandwich box, then.'

'There's isn't room.'

'There is if you take the sandwiches out.'

'OK, don't look.'

'Fuck's sake, Eve. As if I'm interested.'

By the time I've finished, Charlie's eaten all the sandwiches and half the chocolate bar too. 'What the hell?' I ask, zipping myself up.

'Preventative measure. When the moment comes, I don't want you wriggling about and telling me you need a shit.'

'Fuck off, Charlie, you're just greedy. What about you needing a shit?'

'Self-control. In Russia we don't have this culture of instant gratification. Finish the chocolate, Eve.'

'Thanks a lot.'

'Pleasure.' Charlie twists towards me, and grins nastily. 'You're just pissed off because I did your girl.'

'That's history, Charlie. Right now we've got a job to do.'

My voice is steady, but fear is coiling in my guts. I've given up thinking that there's going to be any intervention by Tikhomirov, or any stopping of this thing. The process has begun. All I want now is to do what we have to do and get out fast.

Looking outside, I can see that this is not going to be easy. More and more people are arriving every minute, shouting, jostling and singing. In an hour Red Square will be packed solid. Every few minutes a snowball traces a slushy arc over the heads of the crowd, to be greeted with shrieks and laughter. From further away I can hear ragged cheering, the crackle of fireworks, and the pounding bass of Dima Bilan's latest hit.

'Do you know how we're supposed to get out of here?' I ask Charlie.

'Tolya will take us.'

'So do you know how to get back to the building where we've been staying?'

'Yes.'

'Charlie, talk to me. What's the getaway plan?'

'Tolya knows. Right now I need you to do your job and check for crosswind.'

I inch closer to the right-hand of the two windows with missing panes, making sure that neither I nor the vapour of my breath is visible from below, and gaze along our line of fire. The Lapua round will fly at a declining angle over the roof of the museum, clear the banked snow there by less than half a metre, thread between two monumental nine-teenth-century blocks, traverse two squares and ornamen-tal gardens, and find its target on the pillared frontage of the Bolshoi. Through the Leupold scope I can see people lining up to make their way through the theatre doors into the entrance hall, almost half a mile away. The optics are so fine, and the night air so cold and clear, that I can see the expressions on their faces. I can even read the posters announcing the evening's performance. *Schelkunchik. The Nutcracker.* I lower the scope and everything is miniature again and the Bolshoi a distant white matchbox.

At quarter-past seven our control comes back on air. 'Targets en route, currently ten minutes away from destination. Stand by Echo, Charlie.'

'Standing by.'

Charlie loads, the snick of the AX's bolt action barely audible, and settles theirself, while I briefly aim the Leupold scope at snow-covered bushes five hundred metres away. There's not a tremor, not a flutter of a leaf. We have perfect, windless conditions.

I try to calm my heart. Breathe in, hold for four counts. Breathe out, hold for four counts. Breathe in . . . It's not working. My heart's punching my ribs, my mouth is dry, and my neck aches from peering through the Leupold. I scan the target area. The walkway outside the theatre has been cleared of people. The left and right entrance doors have been closed. A deputation of three men and a woman waits by the centre door.

'Can you confirm head-shot range on that middle door?' Charlie asks me.

'Seven hundred and fourteen point nine.'

'Targets approaching. Two minutes from destination.'

I sense Charlie settling into the weapon, stock to shoulder, cheek to cheek-piece, eye to scope. I can hear their slow, controlled breathing through the headset.

'Car has stopped. Prepare to execute.'

Stechkin is out first, and stands beside the car door for a second as Loy steps out after him. Then both are obscured by bodyguards as they approach the entrance and climb the side steps. 'Wait until the door,' I tell Charlie. 'They'll stop to shake hands.'

Behind the pillars, the group moves fast. Through the scope I catch glimpses of Stechkin, with his asymmetrical gunslinger gait, and the implausible blond swirl of Loy's hair. As they approach the delegation at the door both men halt. Stechkin's profile is in clear sight.

'Send it,' I murmur, my voice weirdly calm, but Stechkin slips from view. From below us, partially muted by the head-set, comes a sound like fireworks, and then there's a thump of feet on the stairs. I freeze, Charlie turns, and a burst of auto-matic fire smashes into their chest. Behind us, weapons levelled, are three men in FSB combat dress. From behind them steps a fourth and obviously female figure, in a black ski jacket and ski mask. Approaching Charlie, who is writhing and gasping in a spreading pool of blood, she pulls off her ski mask and draws her Makarov handgun. 'This is for Kristina, bitch,' she says, and fires a single round between Charlie's eyes. She watches them die, then looks at me bleakly. 'Eve.'

'Dasha.'

The three FSB men help me to my feet. I'm shaking so much I can hardly stand, and when we're joined in the over-crowded octagonal room by Vadim Tikhomirov, I just stare at him.

'Dead?' Tikhomirov asks Dasha, indicating Charlie, and she nods.

'Then we're square,' he tells her.

'We're square,' says Dasha, unzipping her jacket, holster-ing her gun, and giving me a tight, pale smile. 'Thank you all, and goodbye.'

Tikhomirov inclines his head. 'Goodbye, Miss Kvariani.'

As she's leaving, Tikhomirov's phone sounds. He listens for a minute, mutters something inaudible, and shakes his head.

'Where's Vorontsova?' he asks me.

'I don't know.'

'We thought we'd worked out where the second firing point was. I've got a team there right now, but there's no one there.'

She's alive, I tell myself. *She's alive.*

'The good news is that Loy and Stechkin are safely inside the theatre,' he goes on.

'How did you know they were the Twelve's targets?' I ask him.

'They had to be. I knew as soon as I got your report. For which thanks, by the way. You were brave and brilliant, and I could not have asked more of you.' He reaches out his hand, and mindful of the sad, bloodied figure of Charlie on the floor in front of us I shake it.

'And now, while my men clear this place up, I should get you to a place of safety.'

I follow him down the stairs, past the lifeless body of Tolya. When we reach the ground floor he opens a door for me, and then, frowning, closes it again.

'Let's suppose, just for the sake of argument, that there is no second firing point. That the whole idea of two sniper teams is, and always has been, a ruse. A diversion, sold to you in the knowledge that you might be an FSB plant. What then?'

I attempt to pull my shocked and scattered thoughts together. 'Two things, I guess. Firstly, that your intervention here has proved them right, that I was an informer, and secondly . . .'

'Go on, Eve.'

'Secondly, that . . .'

His voice hardens. 'Say it.'

I whisper it. 'That the real attack is happening somewhere else.'

'Exactly. And there's only one place that's likely to be. Where the intended victims are. The Bolshoi Theatre.'

Taking my wrist, he leads me more or less forcibly into a dark, arched passageway, and from there through a massive, studded door into Red Square. It's rammed, and the dazzle of the lights, the blare of pop music and the acrid smell of fireworks envelop me in an instant. Tikhomirov pulls me through the crowd past a set of road barriers, to where a black SUV with FSB insignia is waiting. His assistant, Dima, is at the wheel.

'*Teatralnaya*,' Tikhomirov orders. 'Go fast.'

# 12

Even with the sirens howling, and some very aggressive driving on Dima's part, it takes us almost ten minutes to reach the front of the theatre. The entrance doors are closed, and the sumptuous foyer is silent except for the sotto voce chatter of the front-of-house staff, who surround us officiously as we enter and then stand back respectfully when Tikhomirov identifies himself. He makes a call, and thirty seconds later two FSB officers in dress uniforms hurry down the central staircase, salute, and assure him that all is well, and that all the appropriate security measures are in place. Tikhomirov looks unconvinced and summons one of the theatre managers to take us into the auditorium.

We're led up a short flight of steps to a horseshoe-shaped corridor with numbered doors. 'These are the lower boxes,' the manager explains, opening the furthermost door. 'And this box is always kept in reserve. You're welcome to use it for the duration of the performance.' He withdraws, as unctuous as a courtier, and I look about me. The box is tiny, and upholstered in scarlet. Tchaikovsky's music soars from the orchestra pit, while on stage a Christmas party is in progress, with the dancers in Victorian-era costumes.

It's all so captivating that I momentarily forget why we're here.

Beside me I sense Tikhomirov relax. On the far side of the stage, in a larger, much grander box, all swagged velvet and gold tassels, sit Stechkin and Loy. Stechkin looks inscrutable, Loy appears to be asleep.

'Wait here,' Tikhomirov whispers. 'Sit down.'

He's back two minutes later. 'It's all fine. There are two armed officers outside the presidential box. Nobody can get in.'

I nod. I'm shattered. I'd love to close my eyes and drown in the music, but part of me is wondering, as Tikhomirov is surely wondering, where Oxana is. If Charlie and I were the diversion, what was the plan?

The first act comes to an end, the curtain falls, and the house lights come up. Opposite us Stechkin stands and guides Loy out of sight.

'There's a private reception room attached to the presidential box,' Tikhomirov says. 'They won't be disturbed there.'

'I'm sure they've got plenty to talk about.'

He rolls his eyes and smiles wearily. 'No shit.'

We remain in our seats. Tikhomirov keeps a phone connection open to his officers, but they have nothing to report. He begins to tap his foot and, eventually, he stands. 'Shall we walk?'

'Sure.'

We leave the box and make our way around the long, curved corridor. It's slow going; the passage is narrow and crowded, and several of the patrons are elderly. Halfway round we encounter the house manager, who is speaking irritably into his phone.

'Anything wrong?' Tikhomirov asks.

'Nothing unusual. A woman has locked herself in a toilet stall and passed out, apparently drunk.'

'Where?'

'In the ladies' restroom, downstairs.'

'Take us there, please. Hurry.'

Anxious to oblige, the manager leads us down to the foyer, where a harassed-looking attendant is waiting.

'Show me,' says Tikhomirov.

The restroom is crowded with female patrons, through whom Tikhomirov barges unceremoniously. A bell sounds over the theatre's tannoy system and a voice announces that the curtain will rise on Act 2 of *The Nutcracker* in five minutes. When we reach the locked stall, Tikhomirov puts a broad shoulder to the door and breaks the lock. Inside, a young woman is slumped on the floor. She looks well off, with fine-boned features, little or no make-up, and an expensive haircut. As the manager and I hover behind him, Tikhomirov puts his nose to her mouth, and rolls up one of her eyelids. Over the tannoy, the three-minute bell sounds.

'Well, she's not drunk, and this isn't an overdose.' He rifles through her pockets. 'And what's more, she hasn't got any bag, money or identifying documents on her. Do you recognise her?'

'No,' I say, truthfully. 'I've never seen her before.'

What I don't tell Tikhomirov is that the clothes the woman is wearing, the black jeans, grey sweater, and grey-black Moncler camouflaged jacket, are identical to those Oxana was wearing when she left the building this morning. I pray that I don't look as sick and faint as I feel.

The one-minute bell sounds and Tikhomirov frowns. 'What was that you said to me earlier?'

'When?'

'Ten minutes ago. About Stechkin and Loy.'

'That they . . . had plenty to talk about?'

'Yes. *Yes!*' He gets to his feet, ignoring the unconscious woman and the manager, and runs for the exit, dragging me after him. 'Come on, Eve. Run.'

We tear through the gilded foyer, up the stairs, past ushers and programme-sellers, and back into the corridor serving the boxes. It's almost deserted now; all the patrons have taken their seats for Act 2. At the right-hand end of the corridor, two bulky FSB officers stand outside the door to the presidential anteroom and box. They salute when they see Tikhomirov.

'No one's gone in, General,' one of them says. 'Not a soul.'

'Never mind that,' Tikhomirov barks. 'Has anyone come out?'

'Only the interpreter, sir.'

'Sweet Jesus. Open the doors.'

The four of us burst into the anteroom. It's bright scarlet with a ceiling of tented silk. There's a drinks table, holding open bottles of champagne and malt whisky, and three silk-upholstered chairs. Two of these are empty, the third holds the seated body of Valery Stechkin. He's dead, his neck wrenched unnaturally sideways, and his mouth gaping in a horrible simulacrum of pleasure. The body of the American president, meanwhile, has been arranged in a kneeling posture in front of his Russian counterpart. Loy's neck is also broken and his head has been positioned, face down,

208

in Stechkin's crotch. For several long seconds the four of us stare, incredulous, at the last and greatest work of the artist formerly known as Villanelle.

'Find her,' Tikhomirov whispers to the two men. 'Find the fucking interpreter.'

He closes the door on the dead presidents, pulls out his phone and starts giving orders. Other FSB men arrive at a run and are dispatched around the building. After a few minutes Tikhomirov lowers his phone and stares at me. 'Eve, you need to go. Find Dima. He's in the car outside. He'll take you somewhere safe. Go now.'

It's like walking in a dream, or a nightmare. The corridor seems to last for ever, my steps noiseless on the scarlet carpet. As I step out onto the mezzanine floor the orchestra is playing 'The Waltz of the Snowflakes'. My parents had a scratchy old record of *The Nutcracker*.

Then there's shouting, as six FSB men burst into the foyer from the direction of the orchestra stalls. At their centre, writhing and kicking, is a female figure in a dark suit. It's Oxana and she's fighting for her life. A rifle butt smashes into her head but she fights on, her face bloody, teeth bared like an animal, and with a furious twist of her body manages to wriggle out of the suit jacket that two of the men are holding and sprints for the main door. She makes it, and hurtles down the steps towards the square. Very calmly one of the FSB men steps into the open doorway, raises his rifle and fires an aimed burst. The rounds hit Oxana between the shoulders – spots of red on the white shirt – lifting her momentarily before pitching her onto her face in the wet snow. I try to run to her, screaming now, but my feet won't carry me, hands hold me back, and all that I see is the dark, unfurling flower of her blood.

Of what follows, my memory's fractured. I remember being bundled into a vehicle by men carrying guns, and driven fast through the city. I remember it being very cold when we reached our destination, and being hurried across a court-yard and up a flight of stairs into a small room with an iron bed. I remember letting go. Submitting, finally, to the knowledge that I'm breaking apart.

It's not only Oxana, although it will always be only Oxana. It's the things I've seen and done. I followed her into the *mir teney*, the shadow world, not realising that I couldn't survive there, that unlike her I couldn't breathe its poisoned air. I remember, so clearly, the sensation of riding away with her on the volcano-grey Ducati. Of fitting myself to her back, of holding her tight as we flew into the night. I'd never encountered anyone so dangerous, or so lethally reckless, but she was the only person in the world with whom I felt safe. And now that she's gone, there's nothing left of me.

Oh my love. My Villanelle.

When I finally start to weep, I can't stop.

# 13

An hour after sunrise I'm brought food and coffee on a tray by Dima, Tikhomirov's assistant. He doesn't speak, instead he moves quietly and swiftly. Looking out of the window I recognise the courtyard below and realise that I am inside the Lubyanka complex, the headquarters of the FSB. The door to my room is unlocked; there's a corridor outside with a bathroom, and stairs leading downwards, but I don't go further than the bathroom. I spend the day curled up on the bed, staring at the rooftops and the falling snow. Later, a man in civilian clothes comes in and gives me an injection, following which I sleep deeply. On the second day a female doctor comes in, asks me to undress, and subjects me to a medical examination. I spend a second day lying on the bed, too tired and numbed to think. In the evening there's another injection, and the soft rush into forgetting.

The next morning Dima arrives with my breakfast and stands by the door, his arms folded, as I eat and drink.

'You're going on a driving trip,' he tells me. 'To Perm, fifteen hundred kilometres away. You will be on the road for two days.'

'Why?' I ask. 'And why Perm?'

'You need to leave Moscow. It's too dangerous here, and you will be in safe hands. Also . . .' He looks at me sympathetically. 'We thought you might like to see the city where Miss Vorontsova grew up.'

No such thought has occurred to me but I nod blankly. I have to go somewhere, and it might as well be Perm as anywhere else. Dima takes my breakfast tray, and returns shortly afterwards carrying a suitcase and a winter coat. The suitcase contains new but nondescript clothes, washing things, and a plastic folder of documents.

An hour later I'm sitting in the passenger seat of an unmarked 4x4 vehicle, some kind of Lada, beside a plainclothes officer. Alexei, as he introduces himself, doesn't say much, but radiates tough, unhurried competence. As he swings the Lada through the narrow, slushy streets east of Lubyanka Square he conducts a speakerphone conversation with a woman named Vika, telling her that he will be away on official business for four days, and asking her to take Archie to the vet if his limp persists.

Twenty minutes later we are on a motorway, headed east. The windscreen wipers thump back and forth, and a snow-blurred landscape rolls past, dull grey and frozen white.

'Music?' Alexei suggests, and I turn on the radio, which is tuned to a classical station. A violin concerto is playing, all spun-sugar romanticism, not my sort of thing at all, but I feel the tears running down my cheeks. Alexei affects not to notice. 'Glazunov,' he murmurs, transferring a packet of cigarettes from his tunic pocket to the glove compartment. 'Heifetz recording.'

As the movement ends I wipe my eyes and blow my nose on a tissue, sniffing loudly. 'I'm sorry,' I say.

He glances at me. 'Please. I don't know the details, but General Tikhomirov told us that you did a brave thing for us. A brave thing for Russia.'

Seriously? What the fuck did he tell them?

'Undercover work is hard,' he says, speeding up to overtake a line of slow-moving vehicles. 'It's stressful. We are in your debt.'

'Thank you,' I reply. It seems wisest to leave it at that.

Warm cars always make me sleepy. After a time I close my eyes, and dream of Oxana, rising up out of the steamy Shanghai street, with her cobra gaze fixed on me. I try to reach her but the pinprick of monsoon rain quickly becomes the slap of bullets into our flesh. We fall into the North Sea, and there, suspended in the icy half-dark, are Charlie, Anton, Kris in her velvet coat, and a naked and grey-lipped Azmat Dzabrati, all of them watching as the currents draw us apart until only our fingers are touching, and Oxana drifts into invisibility. I try to call after her, but the seawater rushes into my mouth, and I wake up.

Alexei tells me that I've been asleep for more than three hours. We stop at a service station for sandwiches, coffee and Milka chocolate. Then Alexei fills the Lada with diesel, takes his cigarettes from the glove compartment, and hands me a loaded Glock. 'Five minutes, OK?'

'Sure. Am I in danger?'

'Not at all. But I agreed not to leave you unarmed and unprotected until we reach Perm.'

'Right.' I pocket the Glock, go for a pee in the foul, frozen toilet, and wonder about shooting myself, as I did in Dasha's apartment. Is this my future? Moving from place to place, never settling, never resting, never forgetting? That after-noon we drive for a further six hours in a hissing column of trucks and cars. To either side of the motorway an endless vista of snowbound plains and shadowed forests unrolls beneath cloud-packed skies. At intervals we pass small administrative settlements.

Alexei seems as disinclined to talk about himself as I am. Instead, we listen to music, about which he appears to know a great deal. As each piece starts, he gives me a thumbnail sketch of the work in question. His favourite composer, he tells me, is Rachmaninoff, who saved his sanity in the days and nights following the Dubrovka Theatre siege, his first experience of action, in which a hundred and thirty hostages died.

Alexei points to the passenger-side glove compartment, where among the crumpled cigarette packets and spare Glock magazines I find a cracked plastic case housing a CD of Rachmaninoff's first piano concerto. As the music plays Alexei glances at me, as if to check that it's having the appropriate effect. Perhaps it is, because while I find it complex, and its themes difficult to follow, the act of listen-ing to it occupies me to the exclusion of everything else. It doesn't anaesthetise my grief, but it acknowledges and orders it. It gives it a place.

Evening comes early, bringing with it a sharp wind that scours the snowfields and sends crystalline trails flying through our headlight beams. We stop for the night at a featureless town in the Svechinsky district. Our hostel is a single-storey cinder-block building attached to a motorway service station. The rooms are unprepossessing, but Alexei tells me that the food in the all-night café is good. I try to eat, but I can't swallow. Tears run down my nose and drip onto the plate.

Alexei puts down his fork, passes me a paper napkin and tells me about his home life. He's divorced, and met Vika a year ago at a fellow-officer's birthday drinks. Vika works in the Moscow State University library. She's also divorced, with a football-crazy young son who Alexei says 'has been running wild too long'. They live in a block near Lubyanka Square exclusively occupied by FSB officers and their families. A neighbour takes Archie for walks during the day.

I half listen, grateful not to have to talk, and walk to my room with the Glock weighing down my coat pocket. In the washbag I find a box of sleeping pills. I take one, climb into bed, and listen to the rumble of the trucks outside. Sleep comes blessedly fast.

In the morning we start early, and drive for a further nine hours. Today the sky is clearer, and sunlight pushes through the cloud cover, illuminating the frozen fields and the ice-silvered lakes. The terrain begins to change as we approach the Perm Krai. This is deep Russia, and as the snow's glitter fades the rivers and forests are briefly suffused in soft, glowing pink.

The Azov Hotel is a tiny, one-star place in a side street off Ulitsa Pushkina in central Perm. Alexei pulls up outside shortly after 10 p.m., walks me inside, stamps the snow from his boots, and has an inaudible conversation with the elderly man behind the reception desk.

My room has been paid for, Alexei tells me, and I will be contacted there at some point over the next few days. Reaching into his coat pocket, he hands me a wallet containing a wad of banknotes and a Gazprombank debit card. I probably look as lost as I feel, for Alexei gives me a quick, soldierly hug, squeezes my hand, and wishes me courage. Then he climbs back into the Lada, backs out onto the street, and drives away.

My room is small, with a liver-coloured carpet and a single window overlooking the street. Drawn net curtains admit a thin, diffuse light. There's a divan bed covered by a crocheted blanket, a wooden chest of drawers, and a miniature fridge that throbs so loudly that I turn it off within ten minutes of moving in.

On the windowsill, behind the curtains, I discover a pack of tarot cards. Left behind, I assume, by a previous tenant. I have no idea of the supposed meaning of the cards, but I spend hours sitting on the bed, turning them over one by one, and gazing at the strange, enigmatic images. The angel on the judgement card looks like Oxana. I am the nine of swords, pierced through and through.

This room, and the snowbound streets around the hotel, become my world. I sleep late, eat my lunch at the café over the road, and walk until it gets dark. On my first day I make my way up Komsomolsky Prospekt. I'm glad of the light and warmth of the department stores, but something about the family groups in their coats and headscarves and snow boots upsets me. I feel that I no longer belong among them, and seek out quieter routes in the neighbouring park and along the River Kama.

The Café Skazka is dim and steamy, and the middle-aged couple that run it are friendly, acknowledging me with a smile and a raised hand when I come in, and leaving me to linger over my tea. On the fifth morning their daughter, who works in the café at weekends, refills my cup and offers me a day-old copy of *Pravda*.

I haven't read a newspaper since arriving in Perm, and I've hurried past the shops and bars that have TVs playing, because they always seem to be showing images of the murdered presidents. I'm not ready to learn about it, or to read about Oxana dying, although God knows I've thought about little else. I accept the offer of the paper, nevertheless, touched by the kindly meant gesture, and once I start reading I can't stop.

The lead story, in effect the only story, offers new revelations from 'government sources' concerning 'the crime of the century'. It tells how a transnational anarchist organisation planned the assassination of the American and Russian presidents, and how the Russian security services eliminated the killers in two fierce firefights. There are graphic images of the dead conspirators. Oxana Vorontsova, 'a notorious contract killer known as Villanelle', is described as the leader of the cell, and pictured lying on her back in the snow in front of the Bolshoi Theatre in Moscow, her face and chest dark with blood, surrounded by armed members of the FSB's Alpha counter-terrorist group. An automatic pistol is clearly visible in her right hand. A photograph captioned 'Larissa Farmanyants, the second assassin', shows Charlie's body, torn apart by sub-machine gun fire, lying next to their sniper's rifle at the window of the Nikolskaya tower on the Kremlin wall, 'to which she had illegally gained access'.

On an inside page, where the story continues, there's a TASS news agency photograph, dated seven years earlier, of athletes on the medallists' podium after a pistol-shooting event at the University Games at Ekaterinburg.

Farmanyants, looking wistful, has taken the bronze medal, and Vorontsova, half-smiling, the gold. Both look very young.

According to official government sources, the assassination of the two presidents was very nearly prevented by an undercover operative of the British Secret Intelligence Service, working in collaboration with the Russian security services. The unnamed female officer had penetrated the group, but tragically had been unable to relay the details of the plot to her FSB handlers in time to prevent the assassination. No details are known about this individual's identity or present whereabouts.

The article affirms that the FSB, under the leadership of General Vadim Tikhomirov, has been waging a long, covert war against terrorism and anarchy. 'With such people, there can be no compromise, and no negotiation,' Tikhomirov is quoted as saying. 'Our priority is, and always will be, the security of the Russian people.' In the accompanying photograph he looks sage and reassuring. A little like the actor George Clooney, but steelier around the eyes.

On the sixth day, at eleven-thirty in the morning, I'm sitting cross-legged on the unmade bed, still undressed, turning over the tarot cards, when there's a knock on my door. I assume it's the cleaner, a haunted-looking teenager named Irma who slips fearfully around the hotel with an ancient vacuum cleaner, and I call out to her to give me a minute. When the knock is repeated, I sweep up the cards, wrap the crocheted blanket around me, and open the door an inch.

It's not Irma, but the hotel proprietor, Mr Gribin. 'You have a visitor,' he informs me.

I splash my face with water, dress and walk warily downstairs. Standing in the lobby, facing away from me towards the street, is a woman in a dark coat, with a beret pulled over her hair. Hearing me descend the stairs she turns. She's about forty, with soft, tired eyes. There's a faint smell of cigarettes about her.

'Good morning,' she says, extending a hand towards me. 'I'm Anna Leonova.'

I stare at her.

'I was Oxana's French teacher,' she says. She glances at Gribin, still hovering lugubriously.

I belatedly extend my hand. 'Yes, I know who you are.'

'I wondered, perhaps, whether we might go somewhere and talk.'

'I'd like that.'

We walk to the Café Skazka and order tea. I tell Anna that Oxana spoke of her affectionately, but sadly.

'She was probably the most gifted pupil I ever had,' Anna says. 'Language flowed through her. She had an instinctive feel for it. But she was broken inside. Terribly broken. In the end she did something so terrible that I had to let her go.'

'She told me.'

Anna looks away, her eyes distant. 'I was fond of her, more than fond of her, but I can't pretend I was surprised by what happened. By what she . . . became.'

'Why am I here, Anna? And how do you know who I am?'

The café owner's daughter places a cup of tea in front of each of us. My question is ignored.

'Were you never afraid of her, Eve? Truthfully?'

I pick up my cup, touch my mouth to the scalding tea, and put it down again. 'Never. I loved her.'

'Knowing what she was capable of, you loved her?'

'Yes.'

'Knowing that she could never love you back.'

'She loved me, in her way. I don't expect you or anyone else to understand that, but it's true.'

Anna regards me thoughtfully. 'Did you see the article in *Pravda*, two days ago?'

'I did. And I saw Oxana die. She wasn't holding a pistol. She was unarmed, and they shot her in the back. Not in the chest as the photograph suggests.'

Anna shrugs. 'I believe you. Photographs lie. Even the illusions are illusions.' She interlaces her fingers on the table in front of her. 'I was contacted about you. Told your story. Asked if I could help you make a future for yourself.'

'By whom?'

'I wish I could say, but I can't. This is Russia.'

'Yes, I noticed that.' I try the tea again. It's still too hot.

'I know how unhappy you are, Eve, but will you do something for me?'

I look at her, surprised. Her gaze is soft and unblinking.

'Come with me this evening to the Tchaikovsky Theatre. There's an opera playing. *Manon Lescaut*. It's one of my favourites. I'm sure you'd enjoy it.'

'I . . . Yes, I'd love to. Thank you.'

'Shall we meet there? Seven o'clock?'

'I'll look forward to that very much.'

We sip our tea in silence. It's approaching lunchtime, and a steady stream of customers comes into the café. 'Are you going to have something to eat?' I ask her.

'No, I have to go. But before I do, I have something for you.' From her bag, she takes an envelope and hands it to me. Inside is a small photograph of several girls in school uniform, among them Oxana. She looks about sixteen, and the photographer has caught her off guard. She's half-turning, open-mouthed and laughing. There's something lank-haired and feral about her, but also a childish joy.

'Oh my goodness,' I say, feeling the tears welling. 'That's so precious.'

'Yes. I can remember exactly when it was taken. There had just been an announcement that the whole class had passed the termly exam, and that a girl called Mariam Gelashvili, who had slipped on the ice that morning, had fractured her ankle.'

'Why did you tell me that?'

'Now that I have, is it still precious?'

I slip the photograph back into the envelope. 'She's gone, Anna. It's all precious.'

It's snowing heavily by the evening, and as I step into the sudden warmth of the theatre foyer I'm surrounded by people elated to find themselves in such grand, old-world surroundings. I find a corner to wait for Anna, beside a couple with two daughters. The little girls have been elaborately prepared for the occasion, with giant organza bows in their hair.

Anna catches my attention with a wave. She's wearing a black coat with a fur-trimmed collar that must be decades old, and her mouse-brown hair is pinned up in a French roll. She leads me up the staircase, slipping through the crowds with practised ease. The tea room is splendid, with walls of duck-egg green and russet velvet curtains. Twin chandeliers dispense a soft, yellowish light. We find a corner table, and Anna makes her way to the counter, returning not with cups of tea but two vodka Martinis.

'This is all very generous of you,' I tell her. 'I'm still not sure why you're going to all this trouble for me.'

She smiles over her glass. 'Perhaps we're not so different. We've both lost people.'

I follow her up to the balcony, the Martini racing icily through my bloodstream. Our seats are in the back row. 'Not so expensive,' Anna whispers. 'But the best acoustics. They know me in the box office. I always sit here.'

The lights fall, the curtain rises. The opera is sung in Italian, and I don't try to follow the plot. There are frock coats and cloaks, libidinous men and fallen women. The music washes through me, sweetly sorrowful. I'm carried on a flood tide of vodka and Puccini.

At the interval Anna excuses herself, saying that she has to make a call, so I remain in my seat and gaze out over the crimson and gilt auditorium. Twenty minutes pass and she hasn't returned. Around me, people are returning to their seats, murmuring, consulting programmes. As the house lights go down the buzz of conversation dies. There's a burst of applause as the conductor takes the podium, then the curtain rises to the tremulous sound of a flute. In the near-darkness I register a brief glow of light as the balcony door opens and closes, then see Anna moving along the row towards her seat.

It isn't Anna. The silhouette's wrong.

'*Pupsik.*'

It's her, and I can't speak.

'Eve, *lyubimaya*.' She sits, pulls me to her, and presses my face into her shoulder. She can't be here, and this can't be happening, but I can smell her body and her hair, I can feel the strength in her arms, and her heart beating beneath my cheek. 'I'm sorry, my love,' she whispers. 'I'm so, so sorry.'

I pull back to look at her in the faint light from the stage. She's thinner in the face, and looks tired. Her clothes are plain: a sweater, jeans, snow boots. A parka coat trails over the empty seat next to her.

'I thought you were dead.'

'I know, *pupsik*.'

I start to cry, and she looks anxious for a moment, then pulls a tissue from her sleeve and tentatively holds it out to me. It's such an Oxana gesture that I finally know it's her.

'I did tell you to trust me,' she says.

# 14

That was a year ago. Today the world is a different place. Tikhomirov is president of Russia, and in Europe a new cohort of nationalist leaders has arisen, an advance guard of the new world order, all of them bearing the mark of the Twelve. Oxana and I have new identities and live in one of the outer suburbs of St Petersburg. Our apartment is quiet, with views over a park, which is pretty in summertime and beautiful, if melancholy, in winter. Oxana is at university in the city, studying for her linguistics degree. She is a few years older than the other students, and I suspect that they find her a little strange (on the single occasion that I met her there, two of the young men on the course looked actively scared of her), but she promises me that she is making friends. I divide my time between reading, walking and working for an online translation bureau. Next year, I hope to start a distance-learning course in psychology. There's so much I want to understand.

In hindsight, I marvel at the subtlety and prescience with which Tikhomirov played his hand. I've often thought of that day on the motorway to Sheremetyevo, when he spoke of simulacra. What confused me for a long time was why, if he knew the details of the Bolshoi Theatre assassination plot in advance, as he must have done, he felt it necessary to go through the motions of using me to discover the same information. Why, if he knew what part Oxana was to play, and he must have done to have mounted the operation to fake her death, did he pretend to fall for the diversion?

It was only when Tikhomirov was elected president that everything made sense. The death of his forerunner, Stechkin, was not something that he had been working to prevent, but to achieve. To this end he'd played a long game. Having discovered the Twelve's assassination plan (probably through Richard Edwards, whose capacity for betrayal appears to be limitless), he'd done a deal with them. The Twelve would get their show killing and Tikhomirov, having heroically, but unsuccessfully, attempted to thwart them, would replace Stechkin as president. If Tikhomirov's failure to prevent the assassinations was to be forgiven, following the inevitable investigations, it had to be made to appear that he'd had much less information to work on than was in fact the case. My role was to be his undercover agent, but also his backstop. That's why he let Oxana live. To keep me silent. And if necessary, on message.

Should I have guessed this earlier? Should I have realised that no halfway professional sniper team would have included someone as inexperienced and as temperamentally unsuitable as myself? Probably, but I was so fixated on remaining close to Oxana that I missed it altogether. Perhaps, in the end, it's just as well.

There's much that I don't know, and probably will never know. How did the Twelve find Oxana and me in St Petersburg? Did Dasha betray us, and if not what was the basis of her arrangement with Tikhomirov? More generally, who has the whip hand now, Tikhomirov or the Twelve? Is he their instrument, or are they his? Inevitably, images of that grotesque *tableau mort* in the Bolshoi's presidential anteroom quickly surfaced on the Internet. As a statement of the Twelve's power and reach, and as a warning to other world leaders, it couldn't have been more effective.

In return for the part that we played, knowingly or unknowingly, in the president's rise to power, and for our continued silence and compliance, a monthly payment is made into the bank account that Oxana and I share. The sum is not large, but it meets most of our needs. I save the money I earn from translation for foreign trips. In September we went to Paris. We stayed in a small hotel in the fifth arrondissement, ate our breakfasts in the tiny courtyard and visited the shops around St Sulpice, where Oxana made me try on clothes we couldn't afford. We didn't go anywhere near her former apartment.

Dasha Kvariani is thriving. We met her unexpectedly on Sadovaya Ulitsa, near Oxana's university, where Dasha has opened a nightclub. We went along to the club one evening, and she gave us dinner in the VIP suite, but the conversation didn't flow and Oxana became agitated. We were all too conscious, perhaps, of the weight of each others' secrets.

Winter is here again, and in the park below our apartment the trees are bare and the fountains frozen. I am reading, and Oxana is completing an assignment on her laptop beside me. She is a very competitive student and will be expecting a top grade. Neither of us has spoken for an hour, nor felt the need to. When she finishes her work Oxana closes the laptop, reaches out and takes my hand.

We've often talked about that evening at the Bolshoi Theatre. Not so much about the events in the scarlet ante-room, but about what followed. While the theatrics might have been necessary, Oxana tells me, they were horrible. The blank cartridges, the blood pack under her shirt, all of it. What she remembers most keenly is hearing me scream. At that moment, she remembers, something shifted inside her. 'I could feel what you were feeling.'

Last night I awoke in the early hours of the morning, weeping. I was certain that Oxana was dead, and that the events of the last year had all been a dream. It took almost a minute of her holding me and saying my name to convince me that she was alive. She doesn't experience these terrors herself, but she sees their effect on me and knows that what I need at such moments is to know that she is real, and here.

This morning, we took the Metro to Nevsky Prospekt. The pavements were crowded with shoppers, their breath vaporous in the cold air. We had lunch in Café Singer, above the House of Books, then crossed the road to Zara, where I tried on skirts and sweaters and Oxana bought a hoodie. By the time we came out of the building, the brightness had gone from the sky and the first snowflakes were drifting down. Arm in arm, we walked down to the embankment. We spent a long time there, but no one took any notice of us. We were just two women gazing out over the frozen Neva river, in the fading light of a Russian winter afternoon.

# Acknowledgements

Thanks, as ever, to my agent Patrick Walsh, to Mark Richards and all at John Murray, and to Josh Kendall and the Mulholland team. Alexandra Hackett-Jones read the book first, and her insights were invaluable. Daria Novikova was limitlessly generous with her time and advice, especially in St Petersburg. To my family, who have lived with Eve and Villanelle for more than five years now, my love and thanks.